chapter

1

~ Sonny saw them first. We were climbing
the stairs in B-wing, and I was looking at my
watch, trying to explain why I had to leave,
why I couldn't go to the newspaper meeting.
It was the last meeting of the year—the last
meeting ever, for us—but I had to go home
and make chili.

"I don't even have a recipe," I was telling
Sonny, when he stopped dead, like he'd
walked into a wall. We'd just made the turn
on the landing between floors. I looked at
him. He was frozen stiff, staring up the stairs.
I followed his eyes and saw a guy and girl at
the top of the stairs, making out. They were
really going at it, like they were trying to win
some contest. I hated these people who had

to *perform* for the rest of us. They couldn't go find a closet somewhere?

I glanced back at Sonny. He still hadn't moved, and his face was wide-eyed pale. I didn't get it. Sonny usually didn't even *notice* people making out. His parents were these ex–flower children who taught him that sex was this wonderful, natural part of life. Why was he freaked out all of a sudden by this?

I looked back up at the stairs. Looked at the side of the girl's face, all mashed against the guy's mouth. She looked familiar. She looked like–– I squinted, looking at the perfect blond hair, the red bow, then back at the smushed face.

"Holy shit."

I wasn't thinking, it just came out. It was just so unbelievable. It was Carey Castle up there. Carey Castle. Making out like her clothes were about to burst into flames. If I hadn't seen Sonny looking up at her with his mouth open like that, it never would've occurred to me that it was Carey up there. Girls like Carey just don't go around making out like that. They don't do it. I couldn't believe my eyes.

It just came out.

"Holy shit."

They heard it. Pulled away from each other

and looked down at me staring up at them. It really was her. For real. Carey Castle. With the guy from Echo Falls. Derrick-something.

"How you doin'?" he asked, casual, friendly, smiling.

Carey smiled, too. Like we were being introduced at a party. "Hi, Hale."

I glanced at Sonny, or where Sonny had been. When did he take off? I looked down at the bottom of the stairs.

"Coming to the newspaper meeting?" Carey asked, hugging Derrick's arm, pressing it against one of her breasts. I'd never seen her doing anything like that with Sonny.

"I . . ." I pointed my thumb downstairs for no reason. ". . . don't know."

Derrick? Derrick Krutz?

The voice came booming from up there on the second floor somewhere. I recognized it immediately. Half the school would've recognized it. It was Zoe Mudd. Zoe, my physics partner. Zoe, who wouldn't shut up about me finishing my part of our last lab report.

Carey and Derrick turned their heads.

"Hey, Zoe," Derrick said, with the same casual, ready-for-anything voice he used on me. "How you doin'?"

This was my chance. I quick headed down the stairs.

"What the hell are *you* doing here?" Zoe asked. I looked up, panicky, and saw her for a fraction of a second before I got to the bottom of the stairs and out of view. Did she see me? She loved it when I handed stuff in late; loved asking me about it, reminding me about it, telling other people about it.

I stood at the bottom of the stairs, tried taking a deep breath. The hallway was empty except for pages of a notebook scattered around down near the B-wing door.

It was sad how it was June now, almost the end of the year, and no one stuck around anymore. Three days of classes left, you'd think everyone would hang out after school and celebrate, but that 2:20 bell would ring, and people were gone. By now the senior parking lot was empty. Next week, during exams, there wouldn't even be lunch. And then, a week from Friday, we'd sit in rows of blue robes, waiting for speeches to finish, and we'd throw our square hats in the air, and that'd be it.

I stood at the bottom of the stairs and listened for Sonny. I couldn't see him sprinting all the way down the hallway because he saw Carey up there making out. Sonny wasn't the sprinter type. He was more the sit-there-and-look-pathetic type, and when I saw the bathroom across the hall, I figured that was probably where he was.

"So you guys are a serious *thing* here?" Zoe asked, up above me, her voice bounding down the stairs. I glanced up, half wanting to stick around and listen. No one got on Carey's nerves like Zoe, and it would've been fun hearing Carey try to be nice to her because of Derrick being there. I had to check on Sonny, though, so I stuck my hands in my pockets and walked into the bathroom.

Sonny was in there, standing between the stalls and sinks, looking down at the floor, his head bent sideways like he had a serious neck injury. I didn't move. I hated his broken-neck look. He was like some crushed little bird a cat had brought home and left on the front step.

Carey had dumped him the week before spring break. It'd been three months now. Why couldn't he just get over it?

"He sounds like a jerk," I said.

Sonny looked up, his eyes spacey, far away. "How tall do you suppose he is?"

"Who cares? He's a jerk."

"He looks tall."

I shrugged. Derrick was six-two, had perfect teeth, a tan, and a sports car. Not the kind of guy you want your ex-girlfriend going out with. He went to Echo Falls High School of Science and Math, this magnet school for genius kids. In the fall he was going to Princeton.

"He's a deer hunter," Sonny said. "He hunts with his uncle."

"What? You're impressed he kills innocent animals? I thought you were a vegetarian."

"I didn't say I was impressed."

"You sound impressed."

"I just think he seems well rounded, that's all."

"Because he kills things?"

"You know what I mean."

"Sonny . . ." His neck was bent so far he looked like he was waiting for an ax murderer to take a hack at him.

"He's definitely taller than I thought."

The boom-box voice dropped out of the sky. "It's an optical illusion!"

Sonny jumped. I almost had a heart attack, practically fell over turning around. Zoe was standing just inside the door, her arms crossed.

"You look up the stairs and see a guy in a passionate embrace with your ex-girlfriend. Of *course* he's going to look tall."

Her voice echoed back and forth off the bathroom walls. She sounded like she was trying to get the attention of someone two seats away at a rock concert. I glanced at her as she walked by, ignoring me. She had her long black hair tied back instead of let loose and out of control, and she was wearing flouncy pants and a baggy pink shirt instead of her usual tight, slutty stuff. It felt like a weird dream, seeing her standing there next to the row of urinals.

"She's up there taking him to the meeting."

Sonny looked at Zoe, his mouth dropping open. He'd completely forgotten about the newspaper meeting and quick looked at his watch. He was editor-in-chief and psychopathic about starting meetings on time.

"I need to get up there."

"What. Forget it," I told him.

Zoe walked over to him. She was a little shorter than Sonny but looked like she could take him in an arm-wrestle. "He's right. You don't want to go up there. What if she reaches over and starts massaging his knee? You don't want to be there for that."

I didn't see why she had to bring up knees. "Just cancel."

Sonny shook his head, his brows locked in a knot; he looked like a little kid trying to do long division. "It's the last meeting of the year. I can't cancel."

"Then get this guy to do it," Zoe said, waving a thumb, not even looking at me.

I checked my watch, already shaking my head.

Zoe looked over her shoulder. "You're on the newspaper, right? You run the meeting."

"I can't."

"Why not?"

"I've got to go home."

"You can't spare thirty minutes?"

"I've got to do something."

"Thirty minutes to help a friend."

"Will you—"

"What could be so important?"

"Will you just—"

"He's got to make chili," Sonny explained.

"Sonny—"

"*Chili?*"

I looked at Sonny. "Thanks."

"Tell me you're kidding. Please."

"No, no." Sonny got between us like he was afraid Zoe was going to belt me. "It's for his sister's going-away dinner. It's got to be ready by six o'clock."

"How long do you think it takes to make a bowl of *chili?*"

"Just—"

"Are you planning on growing the beans?"

"Just give me your notes," I said, walking over to Sonny.

"You don't even have a recipe," Sonny reminded me.

"Sonny—" I grabbed at the clipboard he was holding, but he pulled it away.

"I can handle it. Really."

"But you're not going to," Zoe said, and quick plucked the clipboard out of his hands. He looked shocked, like she'd pinched his butt. She held him back with one arm and handed me the clipboard. "Tell you what," she said. "You cover the meeting, I'll finish the lab report."

"Will you stop about the lab report? It's done," I lied, grabbing the clipboard and heading for the door. I checked my watch again as I climbed the stairs. The chili was my stepmother Matilda's idea. She thought it'd be a nice gesture if I made dinner for the going-away party we were having for my little sister, the rock star.

"Chili's Tracy's favorite," Matilda had reminded me. Like I could forget. Like I didn't read about it in *People* magazine. Like Tracy's agent didn't keep telling us about the chili recipes she'd been getting from all over the world.

Dad was worried about me doing dinner. I had a reputation with him for not getting things done on time, and twice at breakfast he'd told me Tracy had an 8:06 flight and we needed to eat by six.

"We'll eat by six, Dad. OK?"

"Do you have the ingredients?" he asked, like one of those cocky prosecuting attorneys who know the guy's guilty as hell.

"I'm picking them up after school," I said, staying calm, pouring milk into my coffee.

"Do you have a recipe?"

"Yes. I have a stupid recipe. OK?" I swung my backpack up on my shoulder and got the door open with my free hand. "Have a nice day."

I was out of breath at the top of the stairs and stopped for a second. This breathing thing had been going on for a while now, and I'd mentioned it in passing to Dr. Lester when I went in for my physical for college. I thought maybe it was asthma, and he could give me some kind of nasal spray. He listened to my lungs with a phenomenally cold stethoscope and just suggested I get some exercise. Dad said maybe I should start riding my bike to school like I did back before I got my license. I'd put my elbow on the table and grabbed my face. "Yeah, right, Dad."

I stood outside the newspaper office and tried taking a deep breath, but it came out more as a gasp. Tina Burns was inside, ranting. She was going to be editor-in-chief next year, because she was the only one who applied. I still wanted to give it to someone else, but Sonny was too honest for that kind of thing.

"We need to give people a reason to read the paper," Tina was saying as I walked in, trying to ignore the faces looking up at me. I hate being watched. The desks were set up in a circle, and Tina was waving her arms around like the head of a marching band. "No one wants to read about the student council. They want to read about individuals. Fights. Arrests. Convictions."

Tina is one of those girls who've read too many biographies about Amelia Earhart. I walked over to the window and waited.

Tina hit her palm against her desk. "We need to find out how many guys are going around carrying condoms. How many people are having unprotected sex."

Carey and Derrick were sitting together over near the blackboard, their desks practically stacked on top of each other. Carey was gently waving a hand, trying to get my attention. I kept my eyes on Tina, acting like I was listening to her.

"Now look, people," Tina blabbed on. "My sources tell me the administration has screwed up royally, scheduling the prom for the last day of classes."

Her sources.

"The last day of classes, you've got kids *primed* to party. It's an invitation to drink. And these are kids who have to take exams Monday morning. It's an administrative nightmare!"

I rolled my eyes and saw Carey gently waving her hand, trying discreetly to get my attention.

"We need to get some of you sophomores over to the prom Friday night. Quote people off the record. Find out if they've had any pre-prom alcohol. Are they renting hotel rooms? Is anyone planning on losing their virginity?"

I rubbed my eyes. I could see Carey over there holding her index finger up like I was her waiter. *Check, please.* I turned and looked out the window and my heart clenched up. Zoe and Sonny were out there. Together. Walking together across the senior parking lot toward his car. Zoe was throwing her arms around, telling one of her stories. What was she saying? What was she telling him? She'd been quiet in physics—just stared into space, wouldn't talk about anything. I'd asked her about Mike, her boyfriend at some college up in Delaware. She just kept staring like she hadn't heard.

Had she and Mike broken up? Was that why she was out there, hitting on Sonny? She didn't even *know* Sonny, except for what I'd told her about him in physics.

Her hands wouldn't stop. She made a chopping gesture and then gave Sonny a push. She was flirting with him. I couldn't believe she was out there flirting with him. Was that why she was so pushy about getting me up here to cover the meeting? Had she just been getting rid of me?

They reached Sonny's car and suddenly Zoe doubled over laughing. She'd done it a few times in physics, usually at her own jokes, and I really wanted to know what was so funny now. I watched as Zoe grabbed the hood of the car to brace herself from the laughing. It got on my nerves, watching her, knowing the way she worked. Sonny wasn't ready for somebody like Zoe. He was incredibly innocent, for a guy. He was what everyone used to pretend guys were like. He was too young for Zoe. Too skinny. Too something.

I turned and headed for the door.

"Hale?"

It was Carey. I kept going and got out to the hallway but then heard footsteps.

"Hale? Hale, wait up."

I looked over my shoulder, still walking. "I'm already late."

Carey skipped along to catch up. "What happened to Sonny?"

I didn't look at her, realized I still had Sonny's stupid clipboard. "What d'you mean?"

"Why wasn't he at the meeting?"

"Prior commitment."

"The reason I'm asking is . . . I get the sense he's having a hard time letting me go."

I stuck my hands in my pockets.

"It just seems as if he's unwilling to accept the fact that we've broken up and I'm dating someone else."

I looked at my watch, took the stairs too fast, and almost got ahead of my feet. Carey kept right up.

"That's why I brought Derrick today," she said, talking faster. "I thought it might be good for Sonny to meet him and know there's a real flesh-and-blood guy I'm going out with."

"Sonny knows about Derrick."

"I know he does. But I'm not sure Sonny *accepts* Derrick."

Was this something from psychology? We both had Mr. Tanner third period. Carey actually did the reading.

"Do you think you could talk to him?"

"Yeah, sure." We were almost to the steel doors at the end of B-wing. I felt like once I got outside I'd be safe.

Carey used the Dorothy-in-Oz voice she usually saved for teachers. "I think it'd really be good for him to talk about it."

"Me, too," I said, banging open one of the doors and walking smack right into Zoe on the other side. I jumped away from her, pulling my hands back, my heart pounding like I'd woken up and found myself on the edge of a cliff.

Zoe laughed.

"Sorry." I turned like a block of wood, avoiding her eyes, afraid she'd seen something. My eyes—she had to see it. Did she realize? Did she know? I felt like I'd accidentally thrown my arms around her and kissed her on the lips.

How could she not notice?

chapter

2

～ "I need a ride," Zoe said, oblivious. "Quick. Come on." She hooked her arm around my arm and pulled me along, waving to Carey, who was still holding the door and watching us like a hawk. "Give Derrick a big, wet kiss from me. Come on. Let's go, let's go."

"Where are we going?"

"Sonny's house," Zoe said.

I slowed down and pulled my arm free. "What for?"

"I need to ask him something."

"Ask him tomorrow."

"Oh, come on," Zoe whined.

"Why can't it wait?"

"I'll give you ten bucks."

I looked at her. Zoe lived in one of those houses up on Stanton Hill where money is no object. "Call a cab."

"A cab won't know where Sonny lives."

"Sixteen forty-nine Yeoman Drive," I said, walking fast, trying to get ahead of her.

"Oh, come *on*. It'll take two seconds."

I looked at my watch. "I don't have two seconds."

"Don't tell me it's the chili again."

I walked faster, heading across the senior parking lot. I'd gotten to school late and had had to park illegally in the alley all the way down by the tennis courts.

"You want a chili recipe?" Zoe asked, catching up. "I know how to make chili. I'll write the recipe down on the way."

"That's OK."

"My dad says it's his favorite. Or he did, anyway, back when he was still talking to me."

Two months ago Zoe had gone up to Delaware for the weekend to see Mike without telling her dad. When she'd gotten back he let the air out of all her tires. She'd been riding her bike to school ever since.

"I'll tell you what," Zoe said, pointing at me. "OK, this is my final offer. You drive me over to Sonny's, and I'll make the chili."

"That's OK."

"We can make it right there at Sonny's, and you can take it home with you."

I looked over at the empty tennis courts. It was a beautiful day. Where were all the stupid tennis players? It was depressing, seeing the tennis courts empty.

"Let me pick up my bike," Zoe said, turning back.

I hadn't been listening. "What?"

Zoe was jogging back to school and called out over her shoulder. "Just swing around to the front of the school."

"Forget it!" I called.

"Two seconds!" she hollered, not looking back.

I stood there. Looked at my watch. Looked at Zoe. She had no idea, hadn't noticed a thing. She'd gone to Echo Falls, this magnet school, for two years, she was supposed to be this genius, but sometimes her head was like a brick.

I looked over at the tennis courts. It seemed as if I'd liked her for a long time. Spring break. Christmas. All the way back in September, maybe—I didn't know for sure. I didn't keep track. It didn't matter. Zoe was always going out with some new college guy, and I was supposedly still going out with Clay, even though her family had moved to Colorado last summer and we'd probably never see each other again. Mondays in physics Zoe would tell me about the frat parties she'd gone to and the guys she'd met and the drinking games the guys played and the underwear they wore. She'd asked me once if I wore boxers or briefs, and when I wouldn't tell her she started talking about all these guys and what *they* wore. I tried to ignore her, especially when she started talking about different colors. I didn't want to know there were college guys out there actually wearing black underwear.

Eventually Zoe always made a point of asking about Clay. Had I called, had I gotten any letters, did I have any pictures? It was nice back in September, when the letters were pouring in, three or four a week, but lately I'd had to start lying. Making up letters, making up phone calls, not telling her about the church Clay had started going to because a *friend* in European history thought she might like it. I didn't even have to ask when Clay told me about it, I knew what *friend* she was talking about; Clay had mentioned the *friend* before. I couldn't remember the friend's name, but I knew the friend was tall and had freckles and was showing Clay how to do all this stuff on his computer.

I looked away from the tennis courts and walked over and climbed into the Buick. I stuck the key in the transmission but just sat there, the heat from the vinyl seeping through my pants. I couldn't see Clay going to church. She used to wear all black and shave her scalp on one side. She just didn't seem like the church type. Or the freckles type. I never would've guessed that Clay would be attracted to freckles.

Of course, I never would've figured Zoe would go for someone like Sonny, either. He was OK looking enough, but he wasn't her type. He was a nice guy. He was voted nicest guy in the senior class. And Zoe liked jerks. The college guys she talked about all had beards and carried lacrosse sticks around at parties. This Mike guy and his friends would drive around in snowstorms, terrifying pedestrians. They robbed vending machines, tackled lampposts, bought inflatable dolls for each other.

"They're assholes," Zoe admitted, laughing.

How could she go from assholes to Sonny? This was a girl who'd gotten drunk at one of these frat parties and went upstairs to some guy's room and took her shirt off in front of him. What if she went over to Sonny's house and did that? What if she walked into his kitchen and pulled her shirt off? Sonny would end up fainting in the middle of the kitchen floor. Knock his head against the edge of a counter.

I looked at my watch, grabbed the steering wheel with both hands, and squeezed tight. I didn't have time to deal with my *own* life, and now I was stuck in this Zoe-Sonny thing. Why'd she want nice all of a sudden?

I pumped the gas a half-dozen times, counted to ten, and turned the key. The engine kicked over, and I pumped the gas to keep it alive. When I got to the front of the school, Zoe was riding her bike in circles around the bike stand, going too fast and concentrating too hard to look up. She could be pretty sometimes, but her mouth was too big and every once in a while she looked like a Muppet. I honked the horn, got out, opened up the back, and winced as Zoe rode her bike off the curb. *Kerplunk, kerplunk.*

"What's this?" she asked, stopping by the windshield and pulling a ticket out from under the wiper. I hadn't seen it.

"What's it look like?"

"Hey, *I* didn't park the car."

"Can we get going?" I took the ticket, got back behind the wheel, and let Zoe deal with the bicycle. I'd gotten about ten or fifteen tickets since spring break, because I'd heard that at the end of the year they didn't bother chasing after seniors. If I was wrong Dad was going to kill me.

"You have a headache?" Zoe asked, climbing in, looking at me rubbing my forehead.

"Just—" I tried to breathe, and smelled a wave of perfume or shampoo or something as Zoe slammed the door. I quick checked the rearview mirror. We sat together like this every day in physics, but it felt weird to see her sitting here in my car.

"Have you ever had a good back massage?"

"Don't start," I said, not looking at her. Zoe was constantly giving these college guys back massages, constantly bragging about it.

"You could use one."

"Just—don't."

Zoe blinked. "So tell me about the chili."

"Just stop about the chili, OK?" I looked over my shoulder, pulled out, and kept my eyes on the road.

"So like—hey, isn't chili like Tracy's favorite food or something?"

I gave Zoe the finger without looking at her. We'd already talked in physics about how the entire world had read the stupid *People* magazine article about the new band Memento Mori and its seventeen-year-old lead singer who loved chili.

"You think you'll miss her?" Zoe asked.

The band was going to be on tour all summer and part of the fall. "What. She's a rock star."

"What does that mean?"

I shook my head and pulled up to the light at Harrison. Zoe reached over and fooled with the radio, and I leaned forward and looked up at the signal. "He doesn't even shave every day."

Out of the corner of my eye I could see Zoe look at me. She turned down the radio, smiling like she was ready to laugh. "What did you say?"

I kept looking up at the light, could feel sweat rolling down my face. "He's not your type."

"Sonny? You don't think Sonny's my type?" The smile got bigger. "What's my type?"

I shrugged, my heart going. "That Mike guy. Up in Maryland."

"Delaware."

"Whatever." The light changed. I raced through the intersection faster than usual, both hands tight on the wheel, keeping an eye out for dogs and police.

"What do you think I'm going to do to him?"

"I'm just saying..." I checked the rearview mirror. "He's not even over Carey yet."

"If he's not over Carey, what are you worried about?"

I just kept my eyes on the road. Zoe slid down in the seat, put her knees up, and pressed them against the dashboard.

"I thought you said she dumped him."

"She did."

"He just finished telling me it was a mutual agreement."

"Two days before spring break Carey told him she wanted to meet at McDonald's. She did all the talking. He kept looking up at the fluorescent lights, couldn't get over how bright they were."

"You were there?"

"He told me about it."

"Why does he say it was mutual?"

"What're you, kidding? Carey's too nice a person to ever dump someone. She convinced him it was mutual."

Zoe chewed on her thumbnail. "And three days later she meets Derrick down in Daytona Beach."

"Sonny thinks it's a miracle. God put them together."

"Wait. Let me guess. You're an atheist."

"He thinks since they met all the way down in Florida it was some kind of cosmic fate."

"You don't believe in fate?"

"What. You think God does everything?" I'd heard enough about God lately from Clay. I didn't want to talk about Him.

"Maybe He's got something in mind," Zoe said, almost whispering. I glanced over at her. Zoe was staring at the glove compartment, her eyes soft, shiny.

"You OK?" I asked, watching the road.

"Am *I* OK? Hey, I'm not the one having a coronary about some beans and ground beef. Am *I* OK? Mr. Nervous Breakdown over here is asking me if *I'm* OK?"

I turned left onto Yeoman. I could feel Zoe watching me but ignored her. Once last year, when we had English together, with Mr. Ziller, Zoe started dancing around, pretending to be a flower in bloom. She was one of these people that sometimes you just have to ignore. I pulled up in front of Sonny's house;

Zoe was still staring at me, like this was some kind of scientific experiment. "What is it?" I asked.

"Are you getting enough sleep?"

I looked over at Sonny's. The Prendergasts' house was small and white and had red flowers in front. They'd been renting it since before Sonny was born. Both his parents worked for nonprofit, save-the-world organizations, and neither of them got paid much. Sonny was going to spend his life paying off college loans.

"I bet you're not getting enough sleep," Zoe said. "Do you know most people suffer from sleep deprivation?"

"I should get going," I said, trying to get her out of the car.

"Aren't you coming in?"

"I have to go to the store."

"I thought we agreed to make your chili here."

"*You* agreed to make the chili here."

"It'll take fifteen minutes."

"I'll make it at home."

Zoe just sat. "You don't want a recipe?"

"You got one?"

She started counting on her fingers. "Pound and a half of ground beef, two green peppers, two onions . . . Let me see. Couple of packages of chili seasonings. Tomato sauce. A little Tabasco. *Ummm . . .*"

"That's OK."

"There's just a couple more things."

"Don't worry about it."

Zoe snapped her fingers. "A little bit of red pepper. And cumin."

"Great. Thanks."

"What's wrong?"

"Nothing."

"Something's wrong."

"Nothing's wrong."

Zoe sat back, crossed her arms. I was never going to get rid of her.

"Look. I need a recipe, not a list of ingredients."

"What're you talking about? It's chili. You chop everything up and throw it in. Sprinkle a little cheese on top."

"Yeah, OK."

"What is *wrong* with you?"

"That's not the way I work! I don't just chop everything up! I need a recipe!"

Zoe looked at me and waved. "Come on."

"I've got to go."

"Just come in a second."

"I don't have the time."

"I'm going to get you a recipe! A real, live recipe!"

"Zoe, would you just—"

She stretched her arm across the seat fast, like she was punching me. I flinched and then stared, frozen, while she yanked the key out of the ignition. "It'll take two seconds," she said, and opened her door. I sat there, watching her walk across the lawn. The car was still in Drive and wouldn't go into Park without the key. I looked back at Zoe and sucked some air into my lungs.

The front door was wide open when I got there. "Sonny?" I could hear the two of them muttering in the little study in the back of the house. The room was small to begin with, then Mr. Prendergast had built floor-to-ceiling bookcases on all four walls. I felt claustrophobic in there, kept looking over my shoulder, expecting shelves of books to collapse on me.

"I know there's one somewhere," Sonny was saying.

"He's going to have a nervous breakdown about this chili."

I rolled my eyes.

"He just wants to get it right," Sonny told her.

"You think he gets enough sleep?"

"Here it is."

I rang the doorbell. "Hello?"

"Thanks. I'll take it to him." Zoe appeared in the hallway, walking toward me, looking down at a Bible-sized book open in front of her. "Chili! Meat chili. Vegetarian chili. Turkey chili. You want chili?" She pushed the book at me. "Here."

I turned the book around and looked down at the recipe for meat chili.

"Maybe you should try going to bed early tonight. Get a decent night's sleep."

"What does *browning* mean?" I pointed to it, to hold my place. "Does that just mean cooking?"

"You don't know what *browning* means?"

"What. It means browning. Making brown. But how brown?"

Zoe stared with her mouth open. "Tell me you're kidding."

"Never mind." I walked around her, back toward the study. Sonny cooked all the time, and he wouldn't make me feel like an idiot. "What's browning?" I asked, walking into the study.

Sonny had the phone in his hand, was hanging it up. He stared at it like it had tried to bite his ear.

"What."

He didn't move.

I couldn't take it. "What."

"She's home," he said, still watching the phone.

"Who? Who's home?"

He kept watching. "Carey."

chapter

3

~ "Wait a second." I didn't get it. Did Carey call him? I hadn't heard the phone ring. "Did *you* call *Carey?*" I rattled my head, still confused. It was like I was watching a little kid shoving his hand in the fire after he'd already burned himself. "Why? Why would you call her? What would you want to talk to her about?"

Sonny sat on the edge of a big leather reading chair, the lamp on the small table next to him shining down on the telephone. He looked dazed, woozy. "I thought I'd get the answering machine."

Was he asleep? In a trance? Under a spell? "You wanted to leave her a message?"

Zoe walked up beside me as Sonny shook

his head and slid back into the chair and pulled his knees up to his chest. "I like hearing her voice on the machine."

I stared, could feel Zoe glance over at me. It sounded like Sonny had done this before, maybe lots of times. No wonder Carey thought he was still hung up on her. A guy keeps leaving messages on your machine, you start to wonder. "How many times have you called?"

Sonny still had his knees pulled up and was drawing on one of them with his finger. "I don't know."

"Three times? Four times?"

"More," Sonny said, not looking up.

I watched him, then spoke softly, like I was talking to an enormous egg. "What do you say in the message?"

Sonny looked up, his eyes big, horrified. "Nothing."

"You just hang up?"

"Yeah."

"You've never said anything?"

He looked like I'd accused him of murder. "No."

I took a deep breath, looked at Zoe. Carey didn't know for sure. She might've suspected Sonny was calling her, but she didn't know anything for sure. She couldn't prove any-thing. I almost laughed with relief.

"What's wrong?" Zoe asked. I looked at her, followed her eyes back to Sonny. He was leaning sideways, like a leaking balloon. There was something he wasn't telling us. He'd been sending Carey telegrams. Death threats. Something.

"What. Sonny, what is it?"

"Derrick."

"What about him?"

"He's there."

"Where?"

"At Carey's."

I stared. "Yeah, right." Carey? Alone at her house with some guy? "Sonny—" I shook my head, then stopped. Remembered Carey and Derrick back at school, at the top of the stairs, making out. It looked like foreplay, the way they were going at it. Did Carey—? Had Carey—? Was Carey—? I looked back at Sonny. "How do you know Derrick's there?"

Sonny stared blankly. "She was laughing."

"What?"

"When she answered the phone. She was laughing."

"Maybe she was watching TV."

"She doesn't watch TV."

"Maybe her mom got home early."

Sonny shook his head furiously. "It's Tuesday."

I stared. My mouth fell open. "Holy shit."

"What's Tuesday?" Zoe asked.

"Holy—" I shook my head.

What's Tuesday?

I turned, avoided Sonny's eyes, whispered, "Carey's mom makes business trips up to Boston on Tuesdays and stays overnight." When Carey and Sonny were going out, Carey wouldn't even let him drop her off at her house on Tuesday nights. Now she was over there with Derrick. Walking around in her underwear, maybe. Did Carey answer the phone in her underwear? Or naked? Was Carey naked when she picked up the phone? It was hard to picture a girl like Carey naked.

"You two think Derrick's going to spend the *night* over there?"

I gave Zoe a look. Even if you're sitting there thinking about your ex-girlfriend sleeping with some guy, even if that's all you can think about, you still don't want someone *talking* about it. It makes it different, hearing the words.

"You guys think they're having sex?"

I winced. "Zoe—"

The phone rang. Sonny reached for it.

"*Wait! Wait!*" Zoe screamed. "What if it's Carey?"

I squinted. "What?"

The phone rang again.

"Calling to see if that was Sonny who just called her."

Sonny looked at me.

"You get it," Zoe said, pointing at me, the phone ringing again.

I couldn't concentrate.

"Tell her Sonny's cleaning out the garage."

"OK, OK."

"You guys . . . ," Sonny whined.

Brrrrnnnggg. The damn ringing was driving me crazy. I reached for the phone.

"No. Tell her he's out gardening. No, tell her he's in the bathroom. That's it! He's in the bathroom!"

"OK, OK," I whispered, like Carey could overhear.

"Taking a shower!"

I jumped, glared over my shoulder at Zoe.

"Just answer it. Come on, hurry up!"

I grabbed the phone. "Hello?"

"*Hale?* Is that you?"

I looked back at Zoe and nodded. "Who's this?"

"This is Carey Castle."

Sonny sat up in his chair. "Hale, let me talk to her."

I turned away from him, faced Zoe.

"In the bathroom," she whispered. Like I was going to forget.

"What are *you* doing there?" Carey sounded offended. "I thought you were in a rush to get somewhere."

"I wanted to check on Sonny. Make sure he was OK."

"Why?" Carey asked in her concerned, animal-shelter voice. She loved all creatures less fortunate than her. "What's wrong?"

Sonny tapped on my shoulder. "Hale."

"He's in the bathroom," I said. "Throwing up."

"Throwing up?!"

"Hale." Sonny sounded like I'd punched him.

Zoe was jumping around, shaking two thumbs up at me. "Beautiful. Beautiful."

"What's wrong with him?" Carey sounded horrified, like I'd told her Sonny was on his deathbed. She loved the possibility of tragedy. "What happened?"

"I think it's that beans-and-rice stuff his parents make. He's been throwing up since lunch."

"Since lunch?"

Zoe started waving her arms, shaking her head. "Are you crazy?" she whispered.

"He seemed OK in journalism." Carey started sounding suspicious.

"It hit him right afterward," I said, but I sounded like an actor who'd forgotten his lines and decided to make something up. Zoe turned away, disgusted. Carey wasn't saying anything. I pictured her over at her house, making hand signals to Derrick.

"Let me talk to Sonny," she said.

"What. Between heaves?"

Zoe gave me a backhand slap on the arm. "Give it up."

"Who's that?" Carey asked.

"Who's what?" I gave Zoe a face.

"Is that Zoe? Is Zoe there?"

"You honestly think that's any of your business?"

"Are you and Zoe dating?" Carey loved gossip. She loved knowing stuff nobody else knew.

"*Dating?* I don't think I know anyone who *dates*. Do you *date*? Are you *dating* Derrick?"

"Going out, then. Are you and Zoe going out?"

"No, Carey. Zoe and I are not going out." Zoe looked up. I turned back toward Sonny, saw him sitting there, his neck broken again. I couldn't take it anymore. "Zoe and *Sonny* are going out," I said, and reached over and hung up the phone.

The whole room was quiet, like after an earthquake. I avoided both of them and looked down at the cookbook I was still holding, my index finger stuck inside, marking the page. "See you."

"Hale," Sonny said.

I looked down at Zoe's black sneakers and held out my hand. "Could I have my keys, please?"

Zoe handed over the keys without a word. I listened as I walked toward the front door. Nothing.

Out in the car I sat breathing, sweating. Without turning my head I looked over at the little white house. Maybe Sonny hadn't thought of it, but it wasn't like I was giving Zoe any ideas. She'd been planning something since she'd walked into the boys' bathroom back at school. Maybe it was good, giving Sonny some warning. Letting him think about the possibility of going out with Zoe before she started ripping her shirt off.

I got the car started and headed down toward Bradley. It was weird, thinking about what was going on right this second. Zoe and

Sonny. Carey and Derrick. Every house I went by, there could've been people inside having sex. Pulling socks off. Unhooking bras.

The light turned red as I got to Bradley. I sat there thinking about Carey Castle, with the stupid red bow in her hair, having sex. She just didn't seem the type. There were some girls who seemed like they wouldn't really be all that interested in sex. They seemed like they didn't have the time, like they'd just as soon wait until they got married. Most of the girls I knew were like that. They liked *laughing* about sex or rolling their eyes about sex or even talking about sex, if it was movie sex and involved some actor who could sleep with half of Nebraska if he wanted. But the idea of real sex with a real human being— that didn't seem like something that they spent their time daydreaming about. They didn't go around imagining taking a guy's clothes off. They didn't—

HOOOOONK!

I jumped, looked up, saw the green light. The guy behind me honked again. Like I still hadn't figured out what was going on. I hit the gas, got to the grocery store, brought the cookbook in with me. The recipe called for medium-sized onions, but the stupid store

had small yellow onions and big white onions. I checked the recipe, but they didn't give
you radius or circumference. I got both kinds,
figured I could decide later.

The phone was ringing when I got home.
I threw everything down on the kitchen table
and grabbed it.

"Hi, Haley." It was Matilda, sounding all
chipper and friendly.

"Hi," I said back, flat. Dad had probably
asked her to call and see how dinner was
progressing.

"What's wrong?" she asked.

"Nothing."

Matilda didn't say anything. I could picture her on the other end of the line, going
through a list of things to say. They must
teach you in social worker school how to talk
slowly and think a lot before you say anything. Sometimes it got on my nerves.

"Did you want something?" I asked her.

"You sound a little stressed out."

I looked at the digital clock on top of the
refrigerator. The store had taken longer than
I'd figured. "I'm in the middle of cooking," I
said.

"Do you need any help?" *Have you*

*screwed up again? Do you want me to bail
you out?*

"No, thanks. But I should get going." I got
off the phone.

Everyone thought it was an unbelievably
wonderful idea, me cooking this dinner for
Tracy. Mom had actually called from Chicago to say how proud she was of me.

"For what?"

"For finally being able to celebrate your
sister's success."

Mom thought I was jealous because the
last time she'd come to visit she'd been fawn-
ing over Tracy-the-rock-star and turned and
caught me pretending to stick a finger down
my throat.

"Who told you about the dinner?" I asked
her.

"Your father."

"Oh."

"He thinks it shows maturity."

"I see." *Maturity* was Mom's word, not
Dad's. Dad didn't think maturity was the
problem. He just thought I was psychopath-
ically lazy.

"You have to be ready to grab jealousy by
the tail."

"Right." I nodded. Mom had said this

before. She probably got it out of one of her self-help books. Either that or a fortune cookie. She loved Chinese food.

She didn't get it.

Tracy's being famous didn't bother me. Back when Tracy was twelve I went around telling people she was going to be famous. The reporter didn't mention that in *People,* but it was true. Tracy was a genius; any genius with a voice like that was going to be famous. Tracy *deserved* to be famous. I was happy for her. I could go around saying "I told you so."

What bothered me was how now we were supposed to be one big, happy family. Now Tracy and I were supposed to be friendly, we were supposed to be mature and talk to each other. We'd been fighting for years. For years Tracy'd been pretending I didn't exist. Now she went around smiling at me, like I was one of her fans. Even Mom and Dad were different to each other now when they talked on the phone. Why? For four years they'd hated each other. Now, all of a sudden, they were going to let bygones be bygones? Why couldn't they've worked on the bygones before they got the divorce? Before Dad dragged us down here to the suburbs of Washington?

Why'd they have to wait for their daughter to become a rock star?

I started chopping up the green peppers like I'd seen Matilda do for salads. I don't even like green peppers, but it felt good to be finally getting started. I got out the big spaghetti pot, opened up cans of kidney beans, threw them in the pot, and checked the recipe. There it was again—*brown the ground beef*. I skipped that part, went to the chopping section. Green peppers. Medium-sized onions.

I stopped, leaned against the counter, looked over at the shopping bag. I needed to decide about the onions. What was medium-sized? Which ones were medium, the white ones or yellow ones? Why didn't I ask someone in the store? Why didn't I just ask the vegetable man? Why did I think it was going to be easier to figure it out *now,* all by myself? I shook my head. Dad was right. I needed to stop putting things off, stop trying to avoid things. I needed to just start *doing*.

Bing-bong, the doorbell rang. Some kid, probably, selling cookies or candy bars or newspapers. I marched over to the grocery bag, pulled out the yellow onions, and started cutting into them before I changed my mind.

Bing-bong. Bing-bong.

The onions got my eyes going. I started to sniffle, wanted to blow my nose.

Bing-bong. Bing-bong. Bing-bong. Bing-bong.

I looked over my shoulder, ready to stab this kid. Maybe it wasn't a kid, though. Maybe it was one of Tracy's fans. Or a pushy agent. Or an overnight letter. Or a package . . . Whatever it was, whoever it was, I couldn't deal with it. Not now. I chopped away at the onions, tears flowing down my cheeks.

Bing-bong, bing-bong, bing-bong . . . It was nonstop now. Whoever it was wasn't letting up.

"Will you just—" My hands were drenched in onion juice, and I kept hitting the paper towels with my elbow but couldn't get the roll started.

. . . bing-bong, bing-bong, bing-bong . . .

I wanted to scream. I grabbed the paper towels and tried ripping one off the roller, but the whole thing unraveled down to the floor. I squeezed a clump of paper towels like I was strangling somebody.

. . . bing-bong, bing-bong, bing-bong . . .

I was practically blind with tears and

knocked over a kitchen chair running to the front door.

... *bing-bong, bing-bong, bing-bong* ...

"WHAT?" I screamed, pulling the door open, trying to tear it off the hinges.

Zoe jumped away from the doorbell and hid behind Sonny. "We're going over to Carey's tonight. Wanna come?"

chapter

4

～ "You're what?"

Zoe got her voice back. "We think she'd like some company. We were hoping you'd drive the getaway car."

I looked at Sonny. "What is she talking about?"

"You're better off not knowing. That way they can't charge you with conspiracy." Zoe walked around Sonny and started past me. "Where's the kitchen? Hey, have you been crying? Whew! You know you smell like onions?"

Zoe went on by. I kept looking at Sonny. "You're really going over to Carey's?"

Sonny smiled, embarrassed, avoiding my

eyes. "We're just going to see if Derrick's car is there."

I blinked. "You can't just drive by and look?"

"We did," Sonny said, lifting a shoulder, sheepish. "Zoe thinks they parked it in the garage."

Pots and pans were clanging from the kitchen like Zoe was throwing them at each other.

"What. You're going to break into the garage?"

Sonny shook his head. "The garage door has those panel windows. We're just going to shine a light."

"You're going to go all the way down her driveway?" Carey lived on the rich side of Oakdale, over near Stanton Hill. She had a little forest of trees in front of her house, and a long driveway. "Sonny, that's trespassing."

"You haven't started browning the meat?" Zoe stomped back toward us. "You put the beans in the pot, but you haven't browned the meat? Are you crazy? I thought you were in a hurry. Come on, come on!" She grabbed me by the arm again, pulled me toward the kitchen.

"Zoe, it's trespassing."

"Hey, you opened the door and let us in."

"Carey could get you arrested."

She waved a hand. "My father's a lawyer. Relax." She pushed a frying pan at me. "Take the meat out of the package, start cooking it. Sonny, find some cumin."

I stood there holding the frying pan against my chest.

Zoe started chopping the rest of the onion. "You want to talk about getting arrested. You still have my bicycle in the back of your car. Stealing bicycles is definitely something the police frown upon."

For a second I thought she was lying, but I couldn't remember taking the bicycle out of the car.

"You know what Freud would say?" Zoe asked, scraping the onions into the pot of beans. "Freud would say you kept the bicycle because you secretly wanted me to come over and help with the chili."

"Look. I don't need help with the chili."

"You don't even know how to brown meat! Of course you need help with the chili. Now just shut up, get the meat going, and show Sonny where you keep spices. I have to go to the bathroom."

I watched her leave, then looked at Sonny.

"She went to school with Derrick," he said.

"Yeah, I know." Zoe had gotten kicked out of Echo Falls after her sophomore year and ended up at Oakdale.

"Derrick tried to kiss her at a party," Sonny said.

I was getting the meat out of the grocery bag and stopped. "He *tried* to kiss her? But she wouldn't let him?"

"She said she was too drunk and didn't trust herself."

"Huh." I tore the plastic away from the meat. "She seems to trust herself just fine, lately." I tossed the clump of ground beef into the frying pan and started jabbing it with a fork to break it up.

"She almost started to cry."

I stopped, turned. "What?"

Sonny was reading the label on a little spice bottle. "Back at my house."

"MIND IF I PUT ON SOME MUSIC?" Zoe hollered from the family room.

"What do you mean, cry?"

"I think she was on the verge of crying."

"Why?"

"I don't know."

I shook my head, impatient. "What made you *think* she was going to cry?"

"HEY, DID YOU KNOW YOU HAVE A MESSAGE ON THE ANSWERING MACHINE?"

I looked toward the family room, then back at Sonny. "Why'd you think she was going to cry? Did you see tears?"

Zoe hollered again. "DO YOU WANT ME TO LISTEN TO IT FOR YOU?"

"NO!"

"DID YOU SAY YES?"

The meat was already starting to sizzle. "WILL YOU—"

"I'LL WRITE IT DOWN."

"JUST LEAVE IT!" I screamed, pushing at the meat with the fork and looking at Sonny. "I think she broke up with that Mike guy over the weekend."

"I was talking about tree pollen," Sonny said, still picking up spice bottles.

"What tree pollen?"

"You know. My allergies. I was telling her that every year my dad and I go for allergy shots."

"And all of a sudden she started crying?"

"Almost."

The telephone answering machine tape was playing back in the family room. It sounded like a woman, but I couldn't hear words. "Does Zoe have allergies?"

"I don't think it was about allergies."

The meat sounded ready to explode, and I stirred it around like I'd seen some guy do on a gourmet cook show. A clump of little strings of meat spilled out onto the stove, and I grabbed it and popped it in my mouth. Then I remembered Matilda saying something about raw ground beef, and I wondered if maybe I'd poisoned myself.

"I think you want to listen to this," Zoe said, walking back into the kitchen.

I looked over my shoulder. "Listen to what?"

"The machine," she said, her voice soft, like she was at a funeral.

Immediately I thought: Car accident, train wreck, plane crash. Would they leave a message on an answering machine about that kind of thing? *Your brother's been in a serious accident. We thought you'd want to know.*

"It's from Clay," Zoe said.

"Oh. OK." I stirred the meat, trying to act offhand.

"I saved the message," Zoe said. "I think you should listen to it."

Clay had been trying to get ahold of me for a while now.

"Hello? Hale?"

"Yeah, OK. Is this brown?" I pointed to the meat. "Is that what browning is?"

Zoe wouldn't look at the pan, wouldn't say anything. She reminded me of Matilda. "Clay said in the message you've been avoiding her. You never come to the phone. You never return her calls."

"What. I'm always in the middle of something," I said, looking back at the frying pan, feeling Zoe standing there.

"Are you going to listen to the message?"

"I'll listen to it. Hold on." The meat had gone past brown; it was gray now.

"It's about her prom," Zoe said.

"Uh-huh. OK." I looked for something to do and spotted the pink Styrofoam ground beef package and threw it away.

"She wants you to call her right away."

"Let me just—" I got a plastic-wrapped block of cheese out of the grocery bag and started opening drawers, looking for a grater. I found a metal spatula, wooden spoons, a hard-boiled–egg chopper, a *plastic* spatula, the little pronged corncobs you stick on the ends of real corncobs, but no grater. It was like the earth had opened up and swallowed the grater.

"She's going to it. She's going to her prom."

"Hold on a second," I said, pushing things in drawers out of the way like I was too distracted to hear what she'd said.

"Why not just call her and get it over with?"

"Look. Just—" I slammed a drawer closed and marched across the kitchen, down the hall, and into the bathroom. I locked the door, flipped on the light, dropped the toilet seat, and sat down. *God.* I stared across at the wallpaper—a pattern of little circles in little boxes. It looked like wrapping paper. I leaned forward and braced my elbows against my thighs. The last Zoe had heard, everything was great with Clay. We were writing all the time, talking on the telephone. We were going to use e-mail when we got to college, and there was even the possibility of Clay getting me a job at the summer camp she was going to be working at. I'd made it sound like we were practically engaged.

I grabbed my forehead. My whole face felt on fire. Why didn't Clay just take the coward's way out and write a letter? Send a fax? It wasn't like I didn't know what she was going to say. It wasn't like we needed to *talk* about it. So she was going to her prom with that tall guy from her church, what's-his-name, the one with the freckles. So they were going to start going out. So it didn't last, me here and Clay out in Colorado. So Mom's prediction back at Thanksgiving was right. So why'd I need to call back? What was there to talk about? Why couldn't we just *write* good-bye? Find cards at Hallmark. Didn't they have cards for every occasion?

I tried to take a deep breath and closed my eyes. Out in the kitchen the side door burst open with a squeak. Dad or Matilda.

"Mrs. O'Reilly!" Matilda and I had run into Zoe one time at the mall back at Christmas. Now Zoe was sounding like they were old friends. "Oh, my God! Mrs. O'Reilly, you're pregnant!"

I kept my eyes closed but it didn't help.

"Hale never told me. I can't believe it. When's it due? Is it a boy or a girl? Do you know? Oh, my god. You look so . . . pregnant!"

Matilda laughed and asked Sonny if he could get some things out of the car. "Where's Hale?"

"Hiding in the bathroom," Zoe told her.

"Why?"

Zoe whispered. I cocked my ear like a dog and heard "Clay" and "prom." Shit. She was telling Matilda everything. Matilda had pretty much figured out on her own what was going on, but it was worse knowing for sure that she knew.

Sonny came back in with the groceries and Zoe's and Matilda's voices went back to normal.

"Mrs. O'Reilly, you must be so excited! It's so wonderful. How pregnant are you? You must be so happy! This must be the happiest . . . You must be so . . ."

"Zoe?" Matilda asked.

I opened my eyes.

"Zoe?"

I looked at the door and heard footsteps going back to the family room.

"Zoe?" More footsteps, Matilda following, speaking softly, like she was talking to a baby she was trying to get to sleep. "Zoe, Zoe. It's OK. It's all right. It's OK."

"I'm sorry," Zoe faltered. Was she crying? It sounded like she was crying.

"Zoe. Zoe. Zoe," Matilda said slowly, rhythmically.

"I just—"

"I know, honey. I know. I know. Wait just a second. Let me put on some music."

I stared at the door. Of course Matilda would make sure I couldn't hear. She had this thing about privacy. No one would know anything about anybody, if Matilda had her way. I stood up and leaned my ear against the door. Matilda had put on some piano concerto and had turned it up. It was hopeless. All I could hear were the stupid violins. I looked at myself in the mirror. Were Zoe's mom and dad finally getting a divorce? Two years ago her mom had gone out to Seattle to live with some neurologist. Zoe didn't like talking about her. All I basically knew was that occasionally her mom would call collect and it drove Zoe crazy that her dad accepted the charges.

Had her mom called? Told Zoe her dad wasn't her biological father? Told Zoe she was adopted?

I opened the door slowly, looking down the hall toward the family room. Matilda hadn't turned on any lamps, but some light was falling in from the sliding glass door out to the deck. I could see Matilda's face, pale in the shadows. Her arms were wrapped around Zoe, whose back was heaving with sobs. Matilda glanced up—the bathroom light still on behind me—and waved me away with an impatient flick of her hand, like I was some servant.

chapter

5

∿ I threw both hands up in the air, turned, and skulked into the kitchen. Sonny was crouched over the bean pot, gently tapping on a tilted spice jar. His hippie parents had taught him how to *create* in the kitchen; they had a three-ring binder full of their recipes and were always making photocopies for vegetarian friends.

"What's wrong?" Sonny asked, looking up.

"How should I know? I'm just the cook."

"Zoe seems upset."

"I guess."

"Is there anything I can do?"

"What're you asking me for?"

Sonny just stood there, like he was thinking about it. I'd never seen him look hurt or offended. You'd have to throw a brick in his face to offend him.

I felt like a caged animal, stuck here in the kitchen, not being able to go into the family room. I paced back and forth, looking over at the doorway.

"What do you think of leaving the meat on the side?"

I looked at Sonny.

He pointed to the pot of chili. "In case some of you guys want to go vegetarian."

It still took me a second to realize what he was talking about, and by then the side door had burst open with a squeaky wail and Dad had walked in with his tie undone and a Friday-night bounce to his step, even though it was still Tuesday. He and Matilda were taking the rest of the week off to go up to New York and hear Tracy sing.

"Hey, guys. How's dinner going?" He glanced over at the stove as he headed toward the refrigerator.

"It's going," I said, walking over to the chili pot and giving it a stir. It looked a lot more like chili than when I left it.

"Smells great," Dad said, grabbing a beer and popping it open. "You guys do good work."

I rolled my eyes and looked over at Sonny, who was grating the cheese.

"Hi, honey!" Matilda waddled in from the family room, holding her stomach in front of her. Dad leaned over and they kissed—a real kiss. It must've been something Matilda learned in social worker school—if you're going to kiss, make it a real, open-mouthed one. I had to turn away every time they said hello to each other.

"Can you stay for dinner, Sonny?" Matilda asked, walking up behind me and looking in the chili pot. "Think there's enough for two more?"

I stopped stirring. "For what?"

"I asked Zoe if she could stay, too."

I waited a beat, started stirring harder.

"Zoe?" Dad asked. "Who's this Zoe?" His voice already sounded loose, like a desk with uneven legs; he didn't drink much and tended to get buzzed pretty fast. "Where is this Zoe?"

"She's in calling her dad," Matilda said. "Hale, is it OK I asked her to stay?"

"Whatever."

"Is someone going to tell me who this Zoe is?" Dad asked, between gulps. "Zoe who?"

"Zoe Mudd!" she screamed, walking in.

"Hi, Mr. O'Reilly. How're you doing?" She was talking louder and faster than ever, and when I looked over my shoulder she was holding on to Dad's hand like she was going to yank him across the room. "Did you really write those lyrics?"

"What lyrics?"

"Oh, come on, Mr. O'Reilly. Don't play dumb."

Tracy'd written the music for three of the songs on the Memento Mori album, and she'd asked Dad to write the words.

"They're great lyrics," Zoe told him. " 'Blizzard Life' is my favorite song."

Dad looked over at me. "Is this a setup?"

I shrugged. "Not by me."

"Mr. O'Reilly!" Zoe sounded offended and told Dad about the first time she heard "Blizzard Life" on the radio, how she was sitting on her bed, folding socks, and stopped just to listen. Dad went over to the refrigerator and got another beer, trying to look like he wasn't really paying attention, but being careful not to make too much noise and miss something. Zoe started actually quoting the lyrics, and Dad stood there, sipping his beer, not even looking at her; but then all of a sudden he laughed out loud.

I saw Matilda smile and do this looking-away thing with her eyes. "Dr. Parker found me the name of someone in New York."

Dad looked at her, and you could see the tumblers fall into place. "Oh! Great! That's terrific. So he said it was OK?"

"Fine."

"You're sure?"

"Martin."

"All right, all right." They were going to be up in New York four days for Tracy's concerts, and since Matilda was eight months pregnant, her obstetrician wanted to make sure they had a doctor they could call up there if they needed to. Matilda was thirty-nine and had miscarried last year, so everyone was stressing about this baby.

Of course, Zoe wanted to know everything—why they were going up to New York, how long they'd be there, where they were staying. Matilda went into the whole thing about how the band's manager kept family away, how the band had to travel by themselves and stay at a hotel by themselves. She even told Zoe *where* the band was staying, which was supposed to be this absolutely top secret confidential information.

"Hale's older brother, Tom, is driving down from Cornell for the Saturday show," Dad told her.

"That's great," Zoe said. "You'll have a little family reunion."

"Except for Hale," Dad said, getting another beer out of the refrigerator.

Zoe looked over at me. "You're not going?"

"Hale feels he needs to study for his exams," Matilda said, looking at Dad instead of Zoe.

It was partly the exams starting next week, but it was mostly that Oakdale was having its prom Friday. Back when Matilda was making the hotel reservations, I thought maybe Clay would want to fly in from Colorado and we could go to it. I was an idiot.

"So, Zoe," Dad said, "what school will you be attending in the fall?"

Oh, shit. Here we go.

"James Anderson," Zoe said.

"James Anderson. Is that right?"

The sarcastic edge was already there. I looked down into the chili pot.

"Sonny, where will you be going to school?" Dad asked, fake interest in his voice. He'd known for three months where Sonny was going to college. "Aren't you going to Anderson?"

"Martin." Matilda knew what Dad was doing.

Zoe didn't. "You wouldn't believe it," she said. "Practically half the graduating class is going to James Anderson."

I winced.

"Me, Sonny, Christel Keller, Jerry Oplinger, Carey Castle, Mo Reirdon. Even Greg Blatski got in, because of soccer."

"Even Greg Blatski. Is that right?" Dad drank some beer. "Did you know Matilda went there?"

"Did you really?"

"Martin."

Dad was chugging away at his beer. "From what I understand, your chances of getting accepted are significantly improved if someone from your family has gone there."

Zoe nodded away. "That's what I hear, yeah."

"Martin, let's set the table."

"Of course, if for some strange reason you check the 'no' box when they ask on the application if a family member has previously attended the university, then the admissions office will obviously not give you any of the special consideration you would have received if you hadn't *lied* on your application."

Dad's voice had gotten louder and louder, and there was a gaping silence now that he was finished. Zoe finally kept her mouth shut.

"I think the chili's ready," Sonny said, oblivious, looking over my shoulder into the pot.

I looked at my watch. 6:01. "Where's Tracy?" I asked, still facing the stove.

Matilda cleared her throat. "Tracy called me at the office. She said she's running a little late."

I turned, looked at Dad. "I thought we had to eat by six."

"Haley," Matilda said, trying to keep things calm.

I just stared at Dad. "Didn't you tell me three million times we had to eat by six? The chili had to be ready by six. Don't forget, plan ahead, be organized! Absolutely, positively *has* to be ready by six."

"Hale." Dad's voice was low and serious.

He could've pulled a knife on me—I wouldn't have stopped. "It was going to be the end of the world, it was going to be a stupid nuclear holocaust, if the chili wasn't ready by six o'clock."

"Hale, take it easy," Dad said, trying to use a social worker voice. He was an accountant; he didn't even know there was a social worker voice until he met Matilda.

I walked over and grabbed the grater and clanged it back down on the counter. "Let me know when it's time for dinner."

"Hale."

"Martin," Matilda called.

I took the stairs three at a time, got into my room, and shut the door. I paced around for a while, then lay down on the floor. It felt good, how far away the ceiling was, but then I felt the stomach-falling panic again.

I was going to Willis College. Quaintly nestled in the tobacco fields of North Carolina. Buddy Mitchell called it his safety school. Buddy Mitchell, who never quite got the commutative property of multiplication. Buddy Mitchell, who wrote graffiti on bathroom walls like CAN'T LIVE WITHOUT WEED. Me and Buddy were the only two people from Oakdale going to Willis. He'd asked if I wanted to be roommates. I had to tell him I was allergic to smoke.

I grabbed my face with both hands and pushed my cheeks together like I was gluing them.

Tracy got home. My room was over the kitchen, and I could hear the door, and then Dad said something. Then Zoe screamed something, and everybody laughed, especially

Dad. He was probably on his fourth beer and had no idea he was laughing like a moron.

The phone rang.

I pulled my hands off my face, sat up. Clay? Was it Clay?

Someone answered the phone downstairs. I stood up, went over, sat on my bed. Dad and I were supposed to have a deal about me making my bed, and I thought about doing it while I waited, but I couldn't concentrate. I looked at my watch. It couldn't be Clay. They would've hollered up by now. Wouldn't they have hollered up by now?

A knock on my door.

Shit. My heart felt like I was competing at a track meet. I started to call out but then stopped. What if they thought I was asleep? Or in a coma? I quick slid under the covers and lay down, then felt stupid. We had a privacy deal in our house, where no one would come into your room uninvited. If I kept my mouth shut, I was safe.

Another knock. Louder. Dad. Great. Just what I needed, Dad after four beers, trying to have a heart-to-heart talk with me about Clay. Dad, talking to me through the door, telling me how *these things happen* and I need to be ready to *face things head on*.

I rolled over. Shut my eyes. Then heard the door open behind me.

"What the—" I jumped up, pushing covers out of the way, ready to explode, start screaming about privacy. But it wasn't Dad standing there.

"Hi."

"You just walk in?"

"Oh, come on. You're up here pouting. You're not going to take your clothes off to pout." Zoe wandered over to my dresser and looked at herself in the mirror. "Does my face look fat to you?"

I didn't feel comfortable sitting there on an unmade bed with Zoe walking around, and I got up and stood there with my arms crossed, my heart still going like crazy. Zoe leaned across the dresser to look at a picture of Clay I had jammed into the side of the mirror. I didn't want her to start asking questions, didn't want to stand there talking about Clay, so I just blurted it out.

"She's going to her prom with a guy from her church."

Zoe acted like she didn't hear me, just picked up the bottle of cologne on my dresser, unscrewed the top, and took a whiff. "How come you don't smell like this?" She lifted the bottle up level with her eyes, saw it was full. "You saving it for a rainy day?"

Zoe was still facing the dresser and looked up and caught me watching her face in the mirror. I turned my head like it'd been an accident, looked down at my desk, at the stupid Willis College roommate survey that I'd been trying to finish. Out of the corner of my eye I could see Zoe grab the old baseball off my dresser and start tossing it in the air as she walked over to the window. I kept waiting for her to say something about dinner, kept expecting Dad or Matilda to holler from downstairs. Why wasn't she talking? She was always talking.

"I guess we better get going," I said, finally.

Zoe just stood, catching the baseball, looking out the window. "Relax. I'm not that kind of girl anymore."

Relax? Did she think I was scared she was going to rip her clothes off? "What kind of girl?" I asked, but Zoe didn't say anything. My heart wouldn't let up. "What kind of girl are you?"

The baseball stopped. "The stupid kind."

I stuck my hands in my pockets. "Did you break up with that Mike guy?"

"It was a mutual agreement," Zoe said, her

voice flat and monotone, like a psychopath's before they all of a sudden kill somebody.

"Is that why you were crying?"

Zoe just stared out the window. "Did I tell you my father hates me?"

"Why?"

"I ruined my life," she said, still facing the window.

I looked in the mirror over my dresser and could see the side of her face. "Because you got kicked out of Echo Falls?"

Zoe's mouth opened, then closed, and she turned and found my eyes again in the mirror. She smiled slowly. "Have you ever had a good back massage?"

She knew. I couldn't breathe. She knew—she could see it in my eyes—and now she was playing with me. "I'm going to wash my hands," I said, and walked past her.

They were already eating downstairs, which was fine with me. I didn't want to see Zoe's reaction when Matilda bowed her head and started talking about God. Matilda had decided we needed to start praying before meals, and her idea of praying was bowing her head and talking like she was having a phone conversation. I sat next to Sonny, and Zoe sat across from me, next to Tracy, who'd had her hair styled again. The manager of Memento Mori was this anorexic woman who thought hair was the most important part of music. They spent a fortune giving Tracy's hair these looks.

The sickly over-brown ground beef was sitting in a bowl by itself next to the pot of chili, and everyone was saying how good the chili was without it.

"It's delicious," Matilda said.

"*Mmmm.* I love it," Tracy said. I rubbed my eyes. Tracy loved everything, now that she was a rock star. It'd probably been six months since I'd heard her say she *didn't* love something.

I grabbed the bowl of meat, piled some on my plate, ladled on a couple of scoops of chili. Looked at Sonny, dared him to say something.

"How's the studying going?" Tracy asked. Like she was some older sister taking care of me while Mom was gone.

"It's going," I said, shoveling in chili. For years Tracy and I had hated each other. She never even talked to me.

"Is there any chance you could fly up on Saturday?"

"So all you guys can be together!" Zoe announced, at the top of her lungs. "That's so nice! Isn't that a nice idea!" Zoe looked at me. "Tell you what. I'll finish our lab report. You go to New York."

"What lab report?" Dad asked.

"Hey, if you're trying to catch up, why don't you come with me and Sonny tonight to study for the history exam?"

I looked at Zoe, could feel Dad look at me.

"What history exam?"

"If the three of us study together, it'll go faster, don't you think?"

"No."

Zoe appealed to Dad. "I've got really good notes."

Dad looked at me. "What're your notes like?"

To my plate: "They're OK."

"Can I see them?"

I didn't move, didn't see a way out. Checkmate. I glared at Zoe. "When're we leaving?"

chapter

6

～ "Guess what my heartbeat is."

I looked over at Sonny. He was pressing his fingers into his neck and looking down at his watch, taking his pulse.

"You're not going to believe it," he said. "Take a guess."

We were sitting in my car in the little grocery store shopping center down the street from my house, waiting for Zoe. She'd gone into the Rite-Aid trying to find a flashlight. Ever since we'd left the house Sonny'd been acting like we were sailing some boat to South America and hiking through a rain forest.

"Do you know what the normal heartbeat is?" he asked.

"Sonny. You're walking down a driveway and flashing a light. It's not that big a deal."

"You're the one who said we could get arrested."

I ignored him, looked over at the Rite-Aid, saw Zoe coming out, walking fast, like maybe she'd stolen something. Was she a kleptomaniac? I had no idea, only knew what she told me in physics. And that might've all been made up. There were times, sitting there in labs, when she didn't yell and we had actual conversations, but whenever we talked about her, Zoe would click into fast-forward and change subjects like she was trying to hide something.

I watched her as she headed toward us. She saw me looking and waved.

"There's Zoe," Sonny said.

"About time."

Zoe opened the passenger door and cool night air gushed in. I felt goose bumps, squinted from the interior light as she climbed in.

"Who's got a pocketknife?" Zoe slammed the door closed, and it was dark again.

"For what?"

"For the panty hose. I got an extra pair, in case you wanted one. Come on, let's go."

Was she planning on changing her clothes?

Here in the car? "What're you doing with panty hose?"

"Drive already! Will you drive?"

I pumped the gas, waited for it to seep into whatever it was supposed to seep into, and started the car. I drove slowly through the parking lot as Sonny got out his Swiss Army knife.

"Wow, this thing has everything," Zoe said, fooling with the knife. "I bet you could build a house with this thing."

Sonny laughed a high-pitched, nervous laugh. I rolled my eyes, surprised he wasn't telling her his heart rate. Zoe clicked open the knife blade and started cutting into the black panty hose. I glanced over a couple of times, bit my lip.

"Is this some sort of fashion statement?"

"Sonny and I are going to wear them over our heads."

I stopped the car. "Wait a second. What?"

Zoe grunted, slicing through the panty hose. "Here you go." She held up a torn-off leg for Sonny.

"You mean you're going to pull them down over your faces?"

"That's the idea."

"Like bank robbers?"

"Relax. We're not robbing any banks. Are you going to drive?"

"Zoe—"

Someone honked behind me. I pulled up to the light at Henderson and tried catching my breath, staring through the windshield. "I thought you were just going to shine a light into the garage, to see if Derrick's car was there."

"Yeah, but I figured as long as we were over there we'd try to steal some furniture."

Sonny laughed again. I gave him a look, but it was dark so he didn't notice.

"I don't think this is a good idea."

"Because of a pair of panty hose?"

"You're going to look like criminals."

"It wouldn't be any fun if we didn't look like criminals."

I tried to ignore her. "Sonny—"

"Green light! Green light! Let's go!"

The guy behind me honked again. I felt like tearing the steering wheel off and flinging it out the window back at him, but I just pulled into the intersection, took a left, and drove.

Zoe and Sonny played with the stupid Swiss Army knife, acting like they were sitting alone in the back of a cab. I felt sweat on my forehead. This was a mistake. Why didn't I just stay home? Catch up on math. Physics. French. Instead I was a stupid chauffeur listening to this new laugh Sonny had all of a sudden. Did he like her? Did he like Zoe? Was this his version of flirting? I had no idea. Sonny never talked about girls he was interested in. He didn't tell me he even *knew* Laura Nickels, and then all of a sudden they were sharing an umbrella in the pouring rain at the homecoming game. And then when he started going out with Carey, I didn't even know he and Laura had broken up.

"You're a Boy Scout?" Zoe screamed. "You're kidding. With the uniform and the badges? The whole package?" She fell into Sonny's lap, leaning across him to look at me. "Are you a Boy Scout?"

"No," I said, checking the side mirror.

"I've never known a real, live Boy Scout. Is it true, a Boy Scout is always prepared? Do you carry a condom?"

Sonny giggled. I couldn't believe it. Since when did he giggle? I wiped sweat off my forehead, rolled down the window. Was this a date? Was I crashing their stupid first date? Were they going to start making out? I turned on the radio, trying not to listen to them, but Zoe started screaming again.

"Could you really survive? If you were dumped off in the middle of Alaska?"

I tried breathing through my mouth, stared at the headlights ahead of us. Zoe didn't seem like Sonny's type. I thought Sonny liked straight hair, no breasts, quiet, *demure*. Carey wasn't always quiet, but she was demure. Ladylike. I thought Sonny wanted ladylike.

"What if a bear attacked and tore off globs of flesh and you were bleeding fountains? What would you do?"

We were half a block from Carey's. "Are you guys going to pay attention?"

Carey's house was set back from the road, and through the trees the lights from the house seemed to blink on and off as we drove by.

"See her car?" Zoe asked. "See how she parked over on the side?"

I squinted but still couldn't see anything. The driveway looked like it disappeared into nothing.

"Why would she park all the way over to the side when Mom's not coming home? Why wouldn't she park in the garage?"

"How should I know?" I held on tight to the steering wheel.

"Pull over up there ahead of the streetlight

and kill the lights." Zoe was practically whispering now.

"This is crazy," I said, pulling over.

"Hit the lights! Will you hit the lights?"

I turned off the headlights and saw nothing ahead of us but black, like we were parked on the balcony of a penthouse apartment.

"Put on your stocking," Zoe said, and Sonny started attacking me with his elbow as he tried to pull the stocking down over his head. I pressed myself against the door.

"I don't think it's going to fit," Sonny said. A surge of hope shot through my system.

"Just—pull hard," Zoe said, grunting with effort. It was completely dark, so I had no idea what kind of progress they were making. I realized I was holding my breath, listening to them struggle. It sounded like they were trying to have sex but couldn't get it right.

"It's hard to blink," Sonny said.

Shit. He had the stupid thing on. "You know, it's dark out there. Why do you need stockings?"

"It makes it more authentic."

"You guys." I felt like I was having a heart attack but no one was paying attention. "Why don't we just call?"

"And say what?"

"You can ask to speak to Derrick."

Zoe laughed with her mouth closed; she sounded like she was blowing her nose. "I'm sure Carey would fall for that."

"This is kind of neat, how it squishes your face," Sonny said.

"Ready?" Zoe leaned across Sonny, tapped my arm. "Hey, if we're not back in ten minutes, don't call the police."

"I have a bad feeling about this."

"Oh, come on! Live a little."

"I live enough."

Zoe opened the door and the light went on. My breath caught. They looked dangerous, evil, with these black stockings distorting their faces, mashing their noses in. I felt like I didn't even know them, didn't know what they were capable of doing.

"Start the car if you hear screaming," Zoe said, and blew me a kiss through the stocking as she slammed the door. I sat there, holding on to the steering wheel. The acceptance letter I got from Willis College said everything was conditional upon me completing my senior year and demonstrating "exemplary citizenship."

"Don't get caught drinking," Dad had said when he read that.

I looked in the rearview mirror but couldn't see anything. I tried to take a deep breath. Driving the getaway car for two people with stockings over their heads was probably not Willis College's idea of *exemplary citizenship*. Especially if something happened, like Zoe all of a sudden decided to break into the garage or throw rocks through the windows. Would she do that? She might, if she was mad enough. Or jealous. Was she jealous of Carey? Did she have a secret crush on Derrick? Was she *planning* on doing something? Was that why she wanted the stockings? Did she *plan* on throwing rocks? Slashing tires? Burning the house down?

I wiped more sweat off my forehead, even though it was cool sitting there in the dark with a cross-breeze blowing through. Would Sonny be able to stop her? If Zoe tried to set the house on fire? I thought about it, imagined Sonny trying to deal with somebody attempting to set a house on fire.

"Shit."

I jumped out of the car and walked fast back toward the skim-milk blue light falling from the streetlight. In the distance I saw two headless figures disappear down the driveway. I started to jog but then slowed down when I got to the driveway because it was gravel and screamed *SCRUNCH* with every step I took. I couldn't see a thing and waved a hand in front of me like a blind man without his cane. I thought I heard Zoe's voice up ahead and stopped to listen but then couldn't hear anything. Where'd they go? I pulled my eyes open wide, but the trees hanging over the driveway blocked out any light.

"Hale?" A whisper. Zoe.

"Yeah." I scrunched ahead a few steps until I saw two shapes in the middle of the driveway.

"What the hell are you doing?" Zoe asked.

"Shhh."

"You're supposed to be watching the car."

"The car's fine."

"What if we need a quick getaway?"

"Then I'll go and start the car."

"Did you bring your stocking?"

"Yeah, right."

"You need a stocking."

"Let's just get this over with. OK?"

No one moved. No one said anything.

"I need to talk to him," Zoe said.

"Who?" I turned my head, saw a light from the house.

"We'll be right back. Don't go anywhere."

I stood there, kept turning my head, looking for shadows. Was she trying to lose me?

Did she think I was an idiot? I took a step, knocked into someone coming the other way. Smelled perfume, shampoo. Something.

"Come on. This way." Zoe put her hands on my chest, felt her way to my arm, grabbed it, and pulled me along back toward the street.

"What. What's going on?"

"I want to ask you something," Zoe said, still pulling me along by the elbow. I was nervous and couldn't stop shivering and just listened to our feet on the gravel. My heart flopped around like a fish in the bottom of a rowboat. What was she going to ask me? What did she want to know?

chapter

7

～ "Is Sonny a virgin?" Zoe whispered when we got to the street.

I could feel her breath through the stocking but couldn't see a face. "What do you mean?" I pulled my elbow away, stuck my hands in my pockets.

"What do you think I mean? Is he a virgin?"

"How should I know?"

"He just told me Carey's mom has been going up to Boston for years on Tuesday-night business trips, but Carey never invited him to stay over with her."

"So what?" After Carey dumped him, Sonny had dreams where she'd invite him over on a Tuesday night and cook him dinner and take his hand and lead him upstairs to her bedroom. But even in the dreams something always went wrong. The oven would suddenly melt or Carey would fall out her bedroom window. Something.

"If he didn't come over on Tuesday nights, does that mean they never had sex?"

"I never asked him."

"Carey steals him away from little Laura-what's-her-name and then never has sex with him?"

"How do you know about Laura?"

"You're telling me he and Carey went out for two and a half years and never had sex?"

"Not everybody has sex, you know."

Zoe turned her head toward me.

"Not all the time," I said.

"Is Carey religious?"

"What. You have to be religious not to have sex?"

"For two and a half years? Yeah."

"Maybe she wanted to wait for some birthday, who knows?"

"No wonder he's freaking out about Derrick being up there."

"He's not freaking out."

"They go out for two and a half years, and now she decides she's going to have sex."

"We don't know she's having sex."

"And Sonny's still a virgin."

"Can we get this over with?"

We crunched along the gravel back to Sonny. I tried to step lightly to keep the noise down, but Zoe walked like an elephant.

"We should have a signal," she whispered, the three of us walking through the black tunnel of a driveway, toward the house. "Like Paul Revere. One if by land, two if by sea."

"What are you talking about?"

"In case we get separated."

I got suspicious. "How are we going to get separated?"

"How should I know?" All of a sudden Zoe turned on the flashlight.

"What're you doing?" I screamed in a whisper.

"Can you see that OK? Good. Here's the signal. One means stay put, two means go. OK?"

"Just leave the stupid thing off."

"Oh, come on. You think she's looking out her window, waiting for us?"

"Will you be quiet?"

We came out from under the overhanging trees and the driveway widened and met a big lawn that seemed to glow with a dull light. Lights were on in all the first-floor rooms, but white curtains hid what was going on. Our steps on the gravel sounded like an avalanche.

"Hey," I whispered. "Slow. Soft. Soft steps."

"Don't you think Sonny looks sinister in a stocking?"

"Will you—" I was practically choking.

"You're just jealous," Zoe said. "You wish you had a stocking."

I stopped and faced her. *Shut—up.*

Zoe stood there. "Have you ever heard of a type-A personality?"

I ignored her.

"You need a good back massage. Let me tell you."

I started to say something, then almost walked away, but ended up just breathing.

"Come on, quit stalling." Zoe reached for my arm, but I backed off in time, walked past Carey's red Toyota toward the double-car garage. The row of window panels along the top of the garage door looked black in the dark, but even before I got there I knew Derrick's car was sitting inside. His car was parked on the other side of that door, I could just feel it. When I got to the window and looked at the darkness inside, I knew Derrick's car was in there, part of the darkness.

But then Zoe clicked on the little flashlight

and shined it through the window, and my breath caught like we'd found a dead body.

"Holy shit."

Zoe hit my arm with the back of her hand. "Quiet!"

"This is incredible," I said, staring at the beam of light moving around across the green sports car. Derrick's car. There it was. I thought I'd prepared myself for seeing his car there, thought I'd convinced myself it was going to be there, but it was different actually seeing it sitting there. Which meant Derrick was absolutely, definitely here. He was inside the house, alone with Carey. With his clothes off, maybe. Maybe even making love to her. Right now, while we were standing here in the dark.

Sonny stepped back from the garage. He was still wearing the stocking, but I could see him turn and look over at the house. I didn't know what to say to him.

"Come on, let's get out of here," Zoe said, and grabbed Sonny's arm and tugged. He didn't budge. Zoe looked over at me.

"Sonny?" I called. No reaction. He just stared at the house. Was he wondering what they were doing in there? Was he *imagining* what they were doing in there? Picturing what was going on?

Zoe tugged again on his arm, but Sonny wouldn't move. Zoe reached over and gave me a shove.

"Sonny, let's go," I said. He looked like he was watching something, but when I looked over there wasn't anything to see. It's a weird feeling, breaking up with someone, getting cut off from her life. For over two years Sonny talked to Carey all the time, knew everything about what was going on with her. Knew what she was reading, knew what she had for dinner, knew when her car needed gas, even knew when she was having her period, probably. Now this. Now all he could do was stand outside in the dark and guess.

"Hey, let's go, let's go," Zoe said, tugging again. Sonny stared a few more seconds, then turned.

"I'll be right back," he said, forgetting to whisper, walking along the front of the garage, away from the house.

"Sonny, hold on a second."

"Go get him," Zoe said. I gave her a look over my shoulder.

"Sonny, wait up. Will you wait up?"

Sonny got to the corner of the garage, turned, and headed toward the back. I followed him.

"Stop him!" Zoe said, pushing me from

behind. "Hurry up." She gave me another shove just as I was turning back to look at her, and she nearly knocked me down. I felt like screaming at her but didn't have the breath. What was Sonny doing? I caught up with him halfway down the side of the garage.

"Sonny, come on," I said, grabbing him.

"I want to see something," he told me, pulling slowly away from me. I had no idea he was that strong.

"What? What do you want to see?"

"Her night-light."

"Her what?"

"Up in her room."

Was he going to try sneaking up to her room? "Wait a second. Will you just wait a second?" We were almost to the back corner of the garage. I could see the whole back-yard—the lawn, almost shimmering in the dark, the black rectangles of flower beds, the two pine trees towering into the sky. "Sonny, will you—" I practically tackled him. "Will you talk to me for a second?"

"Talk to him for a second," Zoe said, right behind us.

Sonny didn't stop, but I slowed him down.

"What's this night-light you're talking about?"

Sonny said Carey had this two-foot-tall red Crayola crayon night-light up in her room that she'd had since she was a little girl. "I want to see if it's on."

"Why?"

"I just want to see."

I held on tight. "How?"

"I'm going to walk out there and look up at her window," he said.

"That's all? Just look?"

"That's all," he said, and broke free, walking around a flower bed and across the backyard toward the pine trees silhouetted against the sky.

"Go get him!" Zoe hollered, slapping my arm.

"He's just checking on the night-light."

"Why? Why do you think he cares about the night-light?"

"What. Maybe he thinks if it's on they must be screwing around up there."

"And what if it *is* on? Then what do you think he's going to do?"

I turned, looked at Sonny's shape as he kept walking back, away from the house.

"I told you, he's freaking out."

I kept watching Sonny. It did seem like he was freaking out a little. Would he actually try to do something? Could I stop him if he did? He was a lot stronger than I thought. Plus he had the stupid Swiss Army knife. I couldn't see him actually *using* it on me, but I could see him waving it around.

"He's not rational!" Zoe hollered at me. "Is this rational?"

Sonny turned back to the house and stopped dead in his tracks. The night-light was on. I could tell by the way he'd stopped, the way he held himself there, locked.

"You don't know what he might do."

"Shhh." Sonny was out there muttering something.

"What'd he say?" Zoe asked.

"I don't know. Someone was talking."

Sonny started walking around in a circle, his head bent down, still talking to himself. Zoe was right. This wasn't rational.

"What's he doing now?"

"I think he's looking for something."

"What? What's he looking for?"

"Why don't you go ask him?"

"FREEZE!!!"

I jumped, without breath, my entire insides spilling out, falling down around my ankles. *I'm going to jail. I'm going to jail, I'm going to jail, I'm going to jail.* My mind couldn't get past going to jail.

"Freeze or I'll shoot!"

I froze, then realized the voice was coming from the back of the house and slowly, slowly, slowly—like I was still frozen— leaned my body past the corner of the garage. Everything was dark, but I could make out the silhouette of a man standing at the back door of the house, carrying something. Cop. Had to be a cop. Was he serious? About shooting? Would he really shoot? Didn't they have rules about when to shoot? I was squinting, trying to see what the cop was carrying, when Zoe decided to start flashing the flashlight on and off, trying to signal to Sonny. I spun around, words sticking in my mouth.

"You— Are you crazy?"

All of a sudden, with a click, floodlights filled the backyard like a baseball stadium. What the—? I turned and saw Sonny standing in the middle of the backyard with the stocking over his head. I leaned my head out to check on the cop—it wasn't a cop but Derrick. With a rifle. On his shoulder. Pointed at Sonny.

My throat caught, my lungs froze.

"Move and I'll blow your goddamn head off!" Derrick's face was tucked down against the rifle; he had Sonny in his sights, could blow his goddamn head off any time he wanted. He was a deer hunter. He wouldn't miss. Sonny could be dead. Any second, Sonny could be dead.

Zoe grabbed me from behind and pulled me away from the corner of the garage.

"He'll see you," she whispered in my ear. A real whisper. Finally.

"Put your hands up!" Derrick called out, his voice a little shaky now, like he wasn't quite sure this sinister-looking guy with the stocking over his head was really going to put his hands up. I looked out at Sonny, who slowly lifted his hands over his head. There was a game we played in elementary school where you had to put your hands up, but I couldn't remember the name of it.

"All he has to do is say something," Zoe whispered. "Tell Derrick who he is."

Zoe was right. If Sonny just said something, he'd be OK. *Hi, Derrick. It's only me, Sonny Prendergast.* Something like that.

"Why isn't he saying anything? He should just *say* something." Zoe was getting mad now.

"He doesn't want Carey to know it's him," I whispered.

"He'd rather get shot?"

I shrugged. "Maybe." If he got shot dead,

Carey'd find out it was him back there with the stocking over his head, but by then he'd be dead and wouldn't care.

"This is ridiculous." Zoe stepped out into the light past the corner of the garage. "Time out!" she screamed, trying to pull the stocking off her head but then suddenly throwing her hands up in the air. Right through the stocking I could see her face change, drop open in terror. Derrick had turned the gun on her. And Zoe thought he was going to shoot. Her body was tense, ready to take the shot, and without thinking I reached out, grabbed, and pulled as hard as I could, trying to get her back behind the garage. Even as I pulled I knew it was stupid, knew I wasn't saving her life, knew Derrick might shoot, but by then I had my hands around her and it wasn't like I could change my mind and leave her there.

"What— Moron!" Zoe clawed at me, trying to push away as I pulled. Did she *want* to get shot? I held on and heaved her out of the light and our legs got tangled and we fell back against the side of the garage and slid down to the ground, my elbow smashing against something. "You stupid son of a bitching bastard! You could've gotten me *killed*, you stupid bastard." Zoe was screaming in my face, but I was checking my elbow for blood.

"Freeze! Freeze!! *FREEEEEEZZZE!!!*" Derrick sounded crazed, like he was being stampeded by wild buffalo. I looked up, saw Sonny running for it, moving fast, almost flying toward us. Go, go, go! I held my breath, Zoe grabbed my shoulder. He was going to make it. He was going to make it.

BANG! The gun went off; Sonny went down.

chapter

8

~ Sonny lay facedown on the ground, five yards away, not moving. Was he paralyzed? Dead? Was he dead?

"Oh, my God. Oh, my God. Oh, my God. Oh, my God." Zoe was hysterical. She climbed up on her knees, her hands out in front of her like she was holding a beach ball.

I was behind her, still sitting. You hear about events that change people's lives. Car crashes, boating accidents, rugby injuries. You never think that now, tonight, right this second, you're going to sit and see your life change. Forever.

Sonny lifted his head.

"Don't move!" Derrick squealed, his voice high and panicky. Don't move or what? He'd shoot him again? Sonny tried to get up, look-ing down at his body and patting himself all over like he was checking for his wallet. Was he trying to find where he'd been hit? I'd seen movies like that, where guys got shot but didn't know it and took a couple of steps and collapsed in a pool of blood.

Zoe jumped out to help Sonny as he got on his legs.

"Freeze!" Derrick called, back in control of his voice, but in two steps Zoe had Sonny past the corner of the garage, safe.

"Are you OK? Are you OK?" she asked, her arm around Sonny's waist, trying to sup-port him.

"I don't know," Sonny said, knocking mud off his shirt from where he landed in the flower bed. I stared, looking for blood.

"Have you been *shot?*" Zoe asked, out of patience.

"I don't think so," Sonny said, still looking down, checking for holes. "I think I tripped."

I pulled them along toward the front of the garage, looking back at where Sonny had fallen. What'd he do? Trip on the daisies?

"Then you're OK?" Zoe asked him.

"Yeah, I'm OK."

Suddenly Zoe's fist flew into Sonny's chest. "Idiot!"

"Quiet!" I whispered, picturing Derrick running around the corner of the garage, pointing his gun at us. Zoe swung another fist at Sonny, and I grabbed her, held her back.

"I thought you were *dead!*"

"I'm sorry," Sonny whispered.

"Can we get out of here?"

"Dumb stupid idiot." Zoe spit the words.

"Come on, go," I said, almost dragging her. "Go! Will you go!"

Zoe shook my hands off her, stomped along the side of the garage.

"Can we move a little faster?" I asked, pushing them, looking over my shoulder. Everything seemed darker now, after the lights in the backyard.

"Stupid moron," Zoe shouted. " 'Ooh, ooh, can't let Carey know it's me. I'd rather get shot.' Moronic idiot jerk."

"OK. OK. OK." I jogged between Zoe and Sonny. Halfway up the driveway I heard sirens. Oh, my God. My legs turned to liquid lead, my knees ready to buckle.

"Police!" Zoe called, and disappeared into the black. *My life,* I thought, *my whole life is gone.* Then I was running, passing Zoe in a wild sprint for the car. The sirens got louder, sounded like they were coming from every-

where. I made it to the street, my arms swing-
ing, my legs pumping, everything moving
fast, the sirens catching up, each step jarring
my vision, shaking the streetlight. Then no
breath, nothing left. Both Zoe and Sonny
passed me, still wearing their stockings, looking like thieves, assassins. The sirens sounded
practically on top of us. I was terrified but
couldn't breathe, couldn't run. There was the
station wagon, right in front of me—Zoe and
Sonny were already climbing in, but I wasn't
going to make it—saw the cop car, lights
flashing, racing down Murdoch. Oh, my
God. I thought of diving down, crawling under the car, but Zoe left the door open for
me, the interior light on. Shit. My legs were
bricks now. I dragged them to the car and fell
in and slammed the door closed, the interior
light going off as the police car made a swerving turn toward us.

"Down, down, get down!" I yelled, throwing myself down on the seat and landing on
Zoe's back. Sonny was by the other door, his
face in his lap like they tell you to do for
plane crashes. I twisted my eyes up and saw
reflections of the flashing red and white lights
as the siren screamed past us. I wanted to
look but kept my ear pressed against the back

of Zoe's windbreaker, listened to her heart.

"Start the car," Zoe said, her voice rumbling under my ear.

"What?" I was whispering. Like the cops were going to hear us with the siren going.

"Start the car!" Zoe said, pushing herself out from underneath me and trying to pull the stocking off her head. "Start the car and don't turn on the lights."

My hands were shaking and I dropped the keys on the floor.

"Start the freaking car!"

"I'm trying, I'm trying!" I pumped the gas and shoved the keys into the ignition but couldn't get the engine to turn over. *Raaar, raaar, raaar, raaaar.*

"They went down the driveway," Zoe said, looking out the back window. "Let's get out of here. Come on."

"OK! OK!" I hate being rushed, hate pressure. *Raaar, raaar, raaar, raaar.* The engine kept turning and turning but wouldn't start.

"You're flooding it!"

"I'm not flooding it!"

"I can smell gas!"

"Will you shut up!" I could smell it, too, and held my foot off the gas pedal and tried counting to five but only made it to three. I turned the key and the engine roared to life.

"No lights! Go! Go! Go!"

I shifted into gear and rammed my foot on the pedal.

"Turn! *Turn!*" Zoe hollered, pointing toward Murdoch. I was leaning forward on top of the steering wheel, trying to see in the dark. I spun the wheel toward Murdoch, my foot still on the gas. The back of the car skipped sideways along the road and bounced up against the far curb.

"What is *wrong* with you?" Zoe reached down and grabbed the straps of different seat belts.

"OK, OK, OK, OK, OK," I said, talking to myself, trying to stay calm, trying to think clearly. I knew that was how most criminals got caught—they didn't think clearly, they gave themselves away. They drove too fast, they acted funny at home, they left evidence at the scene of the crime. I needed to think, needed to plan.

"Turn on the headlights," Zoe told me.

How'd I forget the headlights? I flipped them on and couldn't believe how much easier it was to see. I held the steering wheel with both hands, feeling like a fighter pilot.

"Take a left on Harden." Zoe twisted

around, looked out the back window. "We'll go to that diner across from the Rite-Aid. Just hang out."

Zoe sounded like she was used to this. I looked at her. She turned and our eyes met.

"What're you looking at?"

"What."

Zoe glanced away. "Stop sign! *Stop sign!*"

I looked, slammed on the brakes—skidded into the middle of the intersection as a car honked, headlights flashing from the right, shining at us, aiming right at us, then swerving. I sat there stunned as the car went by, still honking. I breathed short, gaspy breaths, as if I'd just broken through the ice into deep water.

"I heard the bullet whistle," Sonny said in a calm monotone, like he was under hypnosis.

"Do you think we could get out of the middle of the road?" Zoe asked, sounding exhausted. I pulled through the intersection and drove along under the speed limit.

"How close does a bullet have to be to hear it whistle?" Sonny asked, still spacey.

"I don't care," Zoe told him.

"I wonder if it went right by my ear."

"I really don't want to hear about it." Zoe slouched down in the seat. We drove along in quiet for a long time. A light rain started falling, and I turned on the wipers, keeping my eyes on the road, looking out for stop signs. When we got to the diner, Sonny climbed out and stood there with his head tilted up, looking at the sky, at the rain falling. I got out on the other side and looked across the roof of the car at him. He sucked in a couple of deep breaths, smiling like he'd finally gotten drunk and liked it.

"Isn't the rain great?"

"It makes my hair curl," Zoe said, holding the plastic bag from the pharmacy over her head as she snuck out of the car and ran toward the diner. Sonny just stood there, breathing, smiling, looking around. I thought he was going to start waving to cars driving by.

"This is amazing," he said, looking at the diner, at the streetlight, at the Rite-Aid. I looked around but didn't see anything I'd call amazing. Sonny held his hand out, palm up, and then brought his hand close to his face, like he was studying how the raindrops landed.

"Want to go inside?" I asked him.

He kept watching his raindrops. "Sure."

When we got to our table, Zoe was ordering a double stack of pancakes from a waitress who looked like she worked too many hours and had too many little kids at home. Sonny slid in on the other side of the booth, the whole front of his shirt smeared with dirt from where he'd fallen. I slid in next to him and ordered a coffee.

It felt uncomfortable, Zoe sitting right across from me like that. In physics we sat next to each other, didn't have to look at each other. I put my napkin on my lap, looked down at the table. Sonny picked up his fork and pressed a finger against one of the tines. Suddenly he flinched, like he was trying to dodge something.

"You OK?" Zoe asked him.

"I was just remembering that feeling."

"What feeling?"

"That I was dead."

Brainwashed. He sounded brainwashed. I glanced at Zoe, felt embarrassed.

"I'm going to die," Sonny said, trancelike.

I looked over my shoulder for the waitress.

"Isn't it funny that this is the first time it's really occurred to me?"

"That you're going to die?" Zoe asked.

Sonny nodded, still thinking, concentrating.

Zoe cleared her throat. "You don't mean, like, now, do you?"

"It wasn't as if I didn't know that one day I was going to have to die. I never believed I was going to live forever. But I think this is the first time I have stopped to think about dying actually happening."

I shivered.

"This is the first time I can imagine it the same way I can imagine driving to school or taking a shower or drinking an orange soda."

"Where's my coffee?"

"Someday I'm going to just stop," Sonny went on. "I'm going to stop, and everything and everybody is going to go on without me."

"I'll be right back," I said, not looking at anybody. I climbed out of the booth and headed back to the latticework thing hiding the little hallway to the bathrooms. It sounded like Sonny'd had one of his moments. He told me once that occasionally he had these moments where life seemed different. Big. *Profound.* A door would open up and he'd see something that made the rest of this seem less serious, less essential. It sounded like getting shot at by Derrick was one of his moments.

I got to the bathroom and stood at the sink, staring at my face. I never had moments. I never had any doors open, never saw any blinding lights that changed my life. Would

getting shot at have done it? Would thinking
I'd been shot have made me different the way
it made Sonny different? He wasn't just spac-
ier. He seemed older. Like different things
would matter now. Things I wouldn't understand.

I really did have to go to the bathroom, I
realized, standing there looking at the mirror.
How can you go for so long without noticing
something like that? I walked over, looked at
my watch a couple of times, waiting to get
finished. Everybody seemed older. Just looking at people in school, in class, in the hallways, in the cafeteria—they all looked ready
to graduate. They seemed already gone, most
of them. Tired of bothering with all the high
school crap. They were looking forward to
college, to getting on with their lives.

When did it happen? When did people get
older? Even Zoe seemed different tonight, the
way she kept her mouth shut and just listened
to Sonny talk about dying. Did something
happen when Derrick pointed the gun at her?
Should I have gone out there? Should I have
let Derrick aim at *me*? When Sonny was getting up after he fell, why didn't I run out and
help like Zoe did? Was I just scared of getting
shot? Scared of dying?

I went back to the sink to wash my hands

and looked back in the mirror. I was eighteen years old. *Eighteen.* Why did I look fifteen? Feel fifteen? I stood there and tried to imagine a guy walking into the bathroom and pointing a gun at my head, but it wasn't quite the same as the real thing. I walked back out and stood behind the latticework, looking at Zoe and Sonny sitting by the window up front. Zoe had her pancakes and was stuffing them in, talking in between bites. Sonny just stared at her, his mouth serious like he was at a funeral. Was he interested? Now that he knew Carey was having sex with Derrick, would he go for Zoe? I watched Zoe stop chewing for a second and stare down at her pancakes. Then she said something quick. Sonny's mouth dropped open like she'd told him she was a princess or a presidential candidate. It looked funny, actually, but then Zoe put her knife and fork on her plate and dropped her face into her hands.

What the—?

I moved forward, my nose up against the lattice. Was she crying? I stared. Her whole body started to shake with sobs. What was it? What was wrong? Sonny leaned across the table, talking to her. He reached over and grabbed one of Zoe's hands and held it with both of his. Zoe kept her eyes covered with the other hand, her body still lurching with gasping sobs. What the hell was going on? What had her crying all the time? Cancer? Did someone have cancer? Did *she* have cancer? Or AIDS? What about AIDS?

"Shit."

If Zoe had AIDS, I wanted to know. I wanted someone to tell me. I walked around the lattice, back toward the table, watching them carefully. Sonny was still talking, looked like he was even half smiling. It couldn't be AIDS, could it? He wouldn't smile about AIDS. Or cancer. Unless he knew about these special new treatments. A cure. Did Sonny know about some cure for cancer? I looked at Zoe. The sobs had subsided, and Zoe was nodding her head and turned away to wipe her eyes.

"Hey," I said, sliding in beside Sonny, acting like I didn't notice anything, couldn't see Zoe's red eyes, couldn't hear her blowing her nose. I just looked down at the coffee the waitress had left for me and sipped it black. Sonny tapped me on the arm. I looked up, saw him smiling.

"Zoe and I are going to drive down to James Anderson."

chapter

9

～ I looked over at Zoe, who was still drying her eyes, and back at Sonny. "Tonight?" I asked, ready to remind them it was Tuesday; there was school tomorrow.

"This weekend. Zoe wants to take a couple of days and see what kind of off-campus housing she can get. I'm going to drive her down."

I looked at Zoe. "You going to tell your Delaware boyfriend about this little excursion with Sonny?"

"I don't have a Delaware boyfriend," she said, still sniffling.

Oh, shit. No more boyfriend. No more boyfriend meant she was available. No more boyfriend meant she and Sonny could do anything. "What about your father? Are you going to tell him about going off for the weekend with some guy?"

"My father will be glad to hear I'm finally planning ahead. Better late than never."

She looked like she was smiling. Was she smiling? I looked at Sonny, who was wiping his mouth with his napkin. Something was definitely going on, but I wasn't going to give them the satisfaction of bothering to find out what it was. I yanked money out of my pocket for the coffee.

"You guys mind walking back to my house?"

Zoe acted hurt. I didn't look at her, just waved good-bye. The rain had already stopped and a cool, humid breeze was blowing. I drove home and parked behind Sonny's car in front of the house. They were going to have sex. They wouldn't go driving down to James Anderson and stay overnight together and not have sex. Not Zoe. Especially with her knowing about Sonny being a virgin and feeling like Carey gave him this raw deal. She'd love it. She'd love having sex with someone like Sonny. She'd love devirginizing him. She'd love—

I waved my hands, trying to push it all

away. Dragged myself up to the house. Dad's and Matilda's suitcases were piled up by the side door for their trip to New York. For four nights I was going to have the house completely to myself, and I hadn't planned any parties, ordered any kegs. None of the stuff you're supposed to do. I felt pathetic.

"How was the studying?" Matilda asked from the kitchen table.

I just looked at her.

"Did you get a lot done?"

"Oh. Yeah." I went over, grabbed some pretzels out of the bag on the counter. Matilda was watching me like a scientist watches a test tube. It felt like we were going to have a *talk*.

"Zoe's nice," she said. "I like her."

I got a glass out of the cupboard, went over to the refrigerator.

"She's cute."

"I guess," I said, pouring some milk. Matilda let me drink it, got out of her chair with a heave-ho, holding her hands under her belly. I avoided looking at her stomach, thought it was scary. If she ever fell down, I could see it bursting open like a watermelon.

"How long have you been friends?"

"Who?"

Matilda took an orange out of a bowl on the counter and began to peel it. "You and Zoe."

"We're just lab partners. I don't even know her."

"I thought you were friends."

"Not— Why? What'd she tell you?"

Matilda gave me a sideways look, like I shouldn't have asked. The social worker *code*. Never tell anyone what anyone said.

"Did *she* say we were friends?"

"Haley—"

"Fine. I don't care."

I went into the family room, but the TV was off. I turned to go upstairs and saw the answering machine blinking. Clay's message. God, I couldn't believe it was still on there, that I could still listen to it. It felt like it was weeks ago when Zoe walked into the kitchen and wouldn't shut up about the stupid message. And here it was. Clay's voice. Right there. All I had to do was hit a button.

I tried pulling some air in my lungs but couldn't get enough momentum. This was the last time I'd hear Clay's voice. Ever. I felt like I was burying her, felt like I should say a prayer, make the sign of the cross. Then I remembered her freckled friend. I remembered what the message was all about, and I quick turned the volume down all the way and hit the message button.

" 'Bye."

I went upstairs, pried my sneakers off, and sat on the side of my bed. What was going on with Matilda, telling me Zoe was cute? Asking how long we'd been friends? What had Zoe told her? And Sonny? What had Zoe told Sonny? And everybody else, maybe. Maybe everybody knew. Maybe the whole world knew why Zoe was going around crying all the time. Maybe *60 Minutes* had done a segment on it.

I stood and started pacing. Was she dying? Was she really for real dying? The thought had crossed my mind before, but only at the paranoid level. There were some things—the house burning down, drowning in the bathtub, Tracy getting shot by some psychopathic fan—some things that I worried about but didn't take completely seriously because part of me knew they were just paranoia. But what if Zoe was for real dying? What if she'd told Sonny because he'd had that stupid mystical near-death experience with the bullet whistling by? Maybe she felt like she could talk to him about it because he'd *almost* gotten killed. He was *almost* dead. Maybe—

I stopped. Heard voices outside. Turned

my head. Them. It was them, coming back for Sonny's car. I ducked down, got on my hands and knees, crawled to the door, and hit the light off. They were talking, but I couldn't make out words. I got up and walked over to the window in the dark and knelt down. They were somewhere under the big tree out by the curb. I couldn't see anything and pointed my ear at the screen.

"Mmmm," Sonny moaned.

I tried to look down there, then quick pointed my ear back at them.

"You should really be lying down," Zoe said.

"Mmmm." Again with the moan. "We could go back to my house," Sonny said.

"Your parents wouldn't mind?"

"Oooo. No."

I turned again and stared. What the hell was she doing out there? Did she have his pants off? Was she—

"Mmmm. That feels great."

I almost hollered down something to get them to stop, but then snapped my fingers: Massage. She was giving him one of her famous *back* massages. Thank God.

I heard Zoe laugh and car doors open and could see some light under the tree where Sonny had parked, but no matter where I moved my head I couldn't see anything specific. Zoe muttered something and they both laughed. Then the doors closed, the engine started up, and they drove away.

I knelt there, frozen in the dark. I hated her laugh sometimes, the way she could sound like a horse with a broken leg. Would she really go home with Sonny? It wasn't even like they'd have to sneak around. Not at Sonny's house. His parents were these radical ex-hippies; they'd let Zoe and Sonny walk around *naked* if they wanted, and then cook them vegetarian breakfast in the morning.

I stood up. Were they going to have sex? Tonight? I'd known it was only a matter of time, that this weekend they were going off to James Anderson and probably would spend half the time having sex, but at least that wasn't until the weekend. I'd have a chance to get used to it.

Tonight, though. I couldn't believe Sonny was going to lose his virginity *tonight*. I didn't really care, except after finding out about Carey, it was tough adjusting to the idea of someone *else* I knew losing their virginity. It seemed like everyone was losing their virginity. The whole world was losing its virginity.

I walked over to my desk in the dark, felt

for the chair, and sat down. Were they really going to have sex? I thought about it for a while, realized it wasn't even the virginity thing that got to me. I'd probably be happy for Sonny if he lost his virginity to Gigi Thompson or Darlene "The Sex Machine" Finucane. Even Brenda Miles. But not Zoe. I *knew* Zoe now. She was practically a friend. You don't want two friends to all of sudden start going around having sex. It felt like they were committing incest.

Of course, if she was dying . . . It's hard to be mad at two friends going around having sex when one of them is dying. *Was* she dying? AIDS? Cancer? It would explain things. It would actually explain a lot of things, if it turned out Zoe was really dying.

I sighed, stood up, paced until my legs got tired, sat back down. I got into bed and tried to get to sleep, opening my eyes occasionally to check the red numbers on the digital clock. In the morning I stumbled into the bathroom and looked at the dark circles under my eyes.

Back in my room I forgot how to get dressed and just sat there for a while on the edge of my bed, holding a sock in each hand.

"Are you OK, Haley?" Matilda asked, looking up from the newspaper as I walked into the kitchen. Dad was over at the counter, sorting out a four-day supply of his vitamins, and he looked over his shoulder. They'd want to talk to me if I stuck around to make a cup of coffee.

"I need to get to school," I mumbled. I told them to have a nice trip, acted like I was in a hurry to get out of there.

I drove right by the 7-Eleven, forgetting to get my coffee, and ended up being the first car in the senior parking lot. I thought about going to the library and doing my math homework but got tired just thinking about it and slouched down in my seat. Just sat there with the radio off, not wanting to move, not wanting to breathe, just wanting to turn to vinyl and become part of the seat cushion.

Cars started showing up, each fitting neatly between the white lines. I slouched down, hoping no one would see me. Sonny and I usually had breakfast together in the cafeteria, but I decided to wait in the car until the first bell rang.

I was even trying to not look over at the main entrance, but I saw them anyway. Sonny was bouncing along with each step, and Zoe was wearing the same clothes she had on yesterday. My heart started beating hard. Were they the same clothes? They had the same baggy look, but I couldn't remember colors. They *might've* been the same clothes. I slid farther down in the seat, watching the two of them through the steering wheel. I knew I shouldn't be watching, felt like I was staring at Janet Koogle in her red minidress or Lisa Overton in those spandex things she wore. I was spying on them. I was spying on my best friends.

They disappeared inside. I sat there, my heart still beating hard, wondering what had happened last night, wondering if Zoe was dying. I took a deep breath. Why not just ask them? Get it over with?

I liked the idea of getting it over with, but when I got to the cafeteria and saw them sitting across from each other, I couldn't figure out the right words. How do you ask someone if they've had sex? If they're dying? I could feel myself sweating. I dumped my stuff on a seat next to Sonny.

"Hey!" he said, sounding all happy to be alive. Was it sex? Did sex do that to him? I avoided looking over at Zoe.

"Want an onion bagel?" I asked Sonny.

Zoe groaned like I'd punched her in the stomach. I looked at her. She had a hand over her mouth, her eyes closed.

"She's not feeling too good," Sonny said.

Zoe looked pasty vampire white. Was she already deteriorating? Just like that? Overnight? I went and got my bagel, thinking if this was going to be a regular thing, Zoe at breakfast, maybe I'd just stop and have breakfast at McDonald's or something. I hated hanging out with couples, hated seeing them smile at each other or kick each other under the table. Especially if it turned out one of them was *dying*.

Sonny had his math book out by the time I got back to the table. Without looking up, he asked me if I'd done the homework.

"You mean at stoplights on the way to school?"

Sonny laughed. He thought everything was funny today. I knew they'd had sex. I gave Zoe a look. She was still sickly pale. I tried smushing cream cheese onto my bagel with one of those stupid flimsy white plastic knives. Sonny was humming softly to himself, and I looked at him closely. They'd had sex. They'd definitely had sex. And Zoe was definitely not dying. You don't go around humming if you've just had sex with someone who's dying.

I couldn't take it anymore. "So long," I said, and felt better as soon as I walked away. If I didn't have to see them, didn't have to be around them, didn't have to hear them hum, it didn't matter how much sex they had. They could go around having orgies as long as I didn't have to hear about it.

I walked through the senior locker bay, eating my bagel, watching people walk by, slam lockers, sit in corners looking like drug addicts. They all acted like it was just another day. Like we'd be doing this for the rest of our lives. It was like no one had told them that in two days classes would be over, that in a week exams would be over and we'd graduate and our lives would be changed forever.

Mr. Wortman was putting problems up on the board when I got there. I sat in my usual spot in the back by the window and watched him. How many years had he been doing this? How many problems had he put up on the board? How many pieces of chalk had he gone through? He wasn't married. Was he a virgin? I looked out the window, depressed because Mr. Wortman might be a virgin.

Sonny got there right at the bell, so I didn't have to talk to him. And when the bell rang to end first period, I quick stalked away to French. Madame Galois was surprised to see me get to class so early and rambled on and on in French about something to do with her house. I felt like telling her I didn't know what the hell she was talking about, that I didn't understand French, that I panicked every time we had oral exercises, but instead I just sat there, nodding my head. You can't tell teachers when you don't understand. If everyone went around telling every teacher every time they didn't understand something, if teachers had any *idea* how much we didn't understand, the good ones would shoot themselves.

I tried to sleep through government, then got to psychology early so I'd be sitting there looking out the window when Carey showed up. I wanted to be ready for her, just in case she thought it had been Sonny standing there in the middle of her backyard with a stocking over his head. She might've suspected all three of us, and I wanted to be ready to look confused, wanted to be ready to act like she was crazy.

I got distracted, though, watching the leaves brushing against each other, thinking about Sonny and his whistling bullet. When I glanced toward the front of the room and saw Carey marching back toward me, I panicked. Did she know? She walked like she knew. She walked like she'd already talked to Sonny about it and he'd told her everything.

Sonny was a pathetic liar. I quick looked back at the trees and tried to remember I didn't know anything. In police shows the criminal always slips up, forgets what he doesn't know.

Just stare at her, I told myself. Just keep looking like you have no idea what she's talking about.

Carey sat in the seat in front of me and leaned across my desk. "We need to talk."

chapter

10

❧ I could've licked her nose, if I'd wanted. "Would you—" I showed her my palms and motioned for her to move away. I didn't appreciate having people's breasts on my desk.

Carey sat up, watching me. She had her hair tied back with a light purple bow with lacy edges. She looked like the kind of girl who wouldn't fool around with her *fiancé.* Hypocrite. I put my feet flat on the floor and pushed my seat back. I hated having people up close next to me like that. My face was bad enough from a distance; I didn't want people seeing stuff they never noticed before.

"Can we talk?" Carey asked.

Act surprised. Don't forget to act surprised. "About what?"

"I think you know."

Shit. My heart was pounding. How do criminals do it? How do they pass those lie detector tests?

Carey cleared her throat. "Is he really seeing Zoe Mudd?"

I didn't move. Was this a trick?

"Hale?"

"Hmm?"

"Is Sonny"—she pursed her lips, smiled coyly—*"dating* Zoe Mudd?"

"Why do think— What're you—"

Carey leaned closer again. Again with the breasts. I looked at the clock on the front wall. "He drove her to school today," Carey said. "I saw them getting out of his car."

I lifted my hands, looked back at her face. "So?"

Carey smiled and looked over her shoulder to see if anyone was listening. "Did they spend the night together?" she whispered.

"Why're you asking me?"

Carey laughed. "Don't you think it's a *riot?*"

"What."

"Sonny? With Zoe?" She kept smiling, waiting for me to get the joke. "I would not have thought he'd go for someone like Zoe."

"What does that mean?"

Carey just smiled at me. *"Zoe?"* She made it sound like an exotic food.

"You don't like Zoe?" Carey hated her.

"I think she's fine," she said, turning sideways and reaching toward her desktop for the shiny blue organizer she had neatly stacked on top of her books. "I just never imagined Sonny would be interested in someone like that?" She made it sound like a question.

"Someone like what?"

Carey shook her head, tearing open the Velcro on her organizer. "It's just so un-Sonny." She laughed, turning organizer pages and making little check marks.

"What's unSonny?" I asked, but Carey kept checking things off in the organizer. "What is it that's so unSonny?"

Carey finally looked up. "Why're you taking this so personally?"

"I just want to know what you define as 'unSonny.' "

Carey shrugged, smiling. "Being that interested in sex?"

"You think that's why he's going out with her?"

Carey laughed. "What's the first thing you

think of when you hear 'Zoe Mudd'?" She went back to her organizer, shaking her head. "I just think it's such a *riot*."

I looked back at the trees.

By the time I got to the cafeteria I could see Carey already leaning across her table, whispering to all her friends, who were smiling in anticipation and burst out laughing when they heard the news. I walked all the way over to the other side of the salad bar to get on line for a couple of slices of soggy Pizza Supreme, but I could still hear them exploding with laughter.

I got my pizza and went over and sat down across from Zoe and Sonny. They were drinking from little cartons of milk and sharing one of Mrs. Prendergast's famous *bean* sandwiches. I yanked off some pizza crust and started chewing on it.

"Sonny's taking me to the prom," Zoe announced, her mouth half full of beans.

I stopped chewing.

"Actually, I suggested it, but I did insist that Sonny let my father pay for everything. We're getting a limousine. I want white."

I bit off a hunk of pepperoni, not looking at her, not listening.

"What is with you?" Zoe asked. "You ever hear the expression *wet blanket?*"

I looked at Sonny. "You should go tell Carey. She'll love it."

As soon as he heard "Carey," Sonny's eyes got big like a basset hound's. "Love what?"

"This whole prom thing." I chewed off another bite. "She thinks it's hysterical you two guys are going out."

"Why?" Zoe asked, fast, her voice cold.

Still not looking at her, I shook my head. "Never mind."

"Look, asshole. Just tell us why it's hysterical."

I looked at Zoe. "You ever hear the expression *your reputation precedes you?*"

Zoe's eyes flashed icy-still and her arm shot up like a startled bird. The milk carton hit me hard in the forehead. "Schmuck."

I dropped my pizza and reached up, feeling for blood on my forehead. I looked at Zoe. "Are you crazy?"

She was already up, walking away.

I looked at Sonny. "Is she—" I stopped and looked down and quick kicked away from the table. The milk carton had landed sideways on the edge of the table and milk had poured over the edge and into my lap.

"Hale," Sonny said, his shoulders sagging like he'd just watched me driving back and forth over a cat.

"What? What do you want?" I was too mad about the stupid milk to deal with Sonny trying to play conscience.

He shook his head and went after Zoe. I looked back at my crotch, tried dabbing at it with some of those tissue-thin cafeteria napkins that don't absorb anything and tear when you try to pull them out of the over-stuffed dispensers. I smelled like a cow. What was the big deal, anyway, that Zoe had to go throwing milk around? What'd I say? I'd mentioned the word *reputation*. Big deal.

I ate the stupid pizza alone and walked to English, my pants dry and stiff and sour smelling. We were doing Robert Frost poems, and Mrs. Blaffer was reading them in her extra-loud voice, like that would help us understand. I kept my eyes down on my book and shook my head. It wasn't like Zoe didn't know she had a reputation. She used to *brag* about her stupid reputation. She told me how Billy Gruggen had built her up to be a nymphomaniac and how it was a tough reputation to live up to. She actually used the word *reputation*. I remembered her using the word.

Now *I* happen to mention the word and all of a sudden she's throwing milk cartons. What happened? She was throwing milk cartons and walking around my bedroom telling me she was not that kind of girl anymore. What did *that* mean? Did she have an operation? Or some kind of spiritual experience, like Sonny last night with the whistling bullet? Was she going to start going around staring at raindrops?

The bell rang.

I tried to take a deep breath. I dreaded physics. Dreaded sitting there next to Zoe the whole class period. What would I say to her?

Maybe she'd cut. I started hoping she'd cut. She'd never cut before, but she'd told me about cutting other classes. It was no big deal to her, cutting a class, and I kept my hopes up until I walked into Mr. Butler's room and saw her over at our table, reading a book.

"Hi," I said, losing my balance and half falling as I climbed up on my stool. Zoe just turned a page, kept reading. She was a fast reader. I'd stopped trying to read lab directions because Zoe would finish them and start the experiment and I'd have to pretend I knew what we were doing. Now I just waited for her to explain everything.

"How's the book?" I asked.

Zoe didn't answer, didn't look up. She just slid some stapled pages across the table.

"What's this?"

"I couldn't sleep last night," she said, still reading.

I looked at the pages. They were my part of our lab report. "What is this? I told you I was going to do it! Tonight. I was planning on doing it tonight."

She turned another page. I sat there, watching her read.

"Why couldn't you sleep?"

Nothing.

"Do you have what's-it-called? Insomnia?"

Still nothing.

"Look, I'm sorry, all right? I shouldn't have said . . . whatever I said. I'm sorry. Maybe I was—I don't know, maybe I was—"

"An asshole."

"Jealous."

Zoe looked up, looked straight at me. Shit. I reached into my backpack and pulled out my textbook. I shouldn't have said anything. Why'd I say anything? I should've just kept my mouth shut.

"Jealous of what?" Zoe asked. I opened the textbook and found a diagram of a bowling ball hitting pins and stared like I was trying to memorize it. "What're you jealous of?"

"Nothing."

"Just say it. Jealous of what?"

Mr. Butler looked over to see what was going on. I kept my eyes on the book and felt like if I concentrated hard enough, I could forget Zoe was there.

"Hale?" Now she was practically whispering. "Would you look at me?"

I was watching the bowling ball and my eyes weren't budging.

"Hale?" She waited and waited but then, finally, turned away. I started breathing again and, when I thought it was safe, glanced over out of the corner of my eye. Zoe was staring off into space. Mr. Butler started talking about the final exam and the rest of us got out our notebooks, but Zoe sat there on a different frequency. She looked like she was traveling in a crowded subway and thinking about her childhood in Nebraska. I kept checking different pages in my notes, acting like I didn't notice her. The rest of us were scribbling away as Mr. Butler wandered around the room, listing things that *might* be on the exam. I hated teachers who did that. Why not just say *Study everything?*

Mr. Butler walked right by our table but didn't ask Zoe why she wasn't writing anything down. It was like he didn't even notice she was sitting there zoned out. Zoe would ace the exam with her eyes closed, but Mr.

Butler was usually the type of teacher who wouldn't let anybody get away with anything, just on principle.

"Can I get my bicycle out of your car?" Zoe asked softly as the rest us were putting our notebooks away.

"Sure," I said, looking up at the clock over the door, watching the second hand, waiting for the stupid bell to ring. I didn't want to get back into the whole jealous-of-what thing, and I didn't even really want to know why Zoe'd spent class imitating a body snatcher.

Pong. Pong. Pong.

The bell. I exhaled relief. "I'll bring it around front," I told Zoe.

"I'll go with you," she said.

"No, no. I can bring it right out front."

"That's OK."

Shit. I grabbed my backpack. Filing out of class, I could see Sonny out there in the hallway.

"He's giving me a ride to a doctor's appointment," Zoe said from behind me.

"What." I shrugged like it wasn't any of my business and gave Sonny a wave. "Hey."

"I'll meet you by your car," Zoe told him.

"I'll bring the bike over," I said, walking fast through the hallway, dodging bodies.

Zoe followed me single file until we got outside. The sky seemed bigger and quieter than usual. We walked alongside each other a few steps.

"The doctor said I shouldn't be riding my bike," Zoe announced. "That's why Sonny's giving me a ride."

Why was she telling me this? I didn't ask, didn't want to get into it. I walked fast and had the key ready for the back door. After a couple of tugs the bike came out, and I got it onto its wheels in front of Zoe and slammed the door.

"See ya."

Zoe watched me walk over to the driver's side. "Don't be jealous," she said, almost whispering again.

"Don't worry." I got the door open.

"If you knew—"

"See you tomorrow." I climbed in and closed the door. It felt like an oven, but I wasn't rolling down any windows. I didn't want to give Zoe a chance to tell me what I didn't know. Not with her sounding sympathetic. What is it about girls that sympathy makes them so talkative? You admit something stupid, like you're jealous, and all of a sudden they want to pour their hearts out to you.

I pumped the pedal a few times and got the car started. I drove down to the line of cars waiting for the light at Harrison and sat there staring up at the signal.

She had a disease. AIDS, maybe. No, not AIDS. Sonny wouldn't have been all smiley like that at breakfast. They wouldn't have had sex last night if Zoe was going around with AIDS. It had to be something else. Something serious. I wasn't up on all the latest diseases, but it had to be some *life-changing* thing. She'd been so weird the last couple of days, it had to be something that made life seem different than it had been before.

One thing was for sure: she and Sonny definitely had sex last night. The way Sonny was humming at breakfast, the way they decided they were going to the prom together, the way Zoe was all contemplative—just being around the two of them, you could tell something was going on. I took a deep breath, shook my head. I couldn't picture Zoe and Sonny together with their clothes off. I couldn't picture them *getting* their clothes off . . . that always seemed like the hard part, when I thought about sex. How do you get from having clothes on to not having clothes on? Do you talk about it? *Hey, why don't we take our clothes off?* Or do you just start taking clothes off and hope the other person doesn't mind?

Cars didn't move fast enough and I got stuck waiting through another light. I slouched and wondered if Zoe and Sonny were sexually compatible. I'd read about it in one of Matilda's women's magazines, how men and women's bodies don't always *match,* and how sometimes one's too fast or the other one's too slow. It was scary stuff— not the kind of thing you should leave around for a teenage boy to read. As if there wasn't already enough to worry about.

Cars were moving along in the right-hand turn lane, and while I was sitting there I noticed Sonny's car go by. With Zoe in the passenger seat. I watched them go, watched the side of Zoe's face as they turned right and headed along Harrison. It was pretty far away, but I could see her really well, like in a movie when the bad guy is looking at the good guy through a telescopic sight. Zoe was talking, but she had her head turned this way, looking out her window. I got goose bumps watching her, like this was the last time I was ever going to see her. I shivered. I didn't like premonitions. Ouija boards. All that kind of crap. I never went to horror movies, never listened to ghost stories, never read about mysterious phenomena. What if it was true, that stuff? What if there really were psychotic killers waiting in showers all over the world? What if you walked down into the basement and really did find the walls bleeding?

I drove home and went through the side door into the kitchen, like I always did, but when I got the door closed I stopped and listened. I'd gotten used to being the first one home, ever since Tom went to college and Tracy became a rock star, but it felt different knowing no one was *coming* home. For four days no one was coming home, and I stood there listening for burglars or small animals. I remembered a dream where a badger or woodchuck came crawling down the steps to the front hall. According to psychology that had to mean something, a woodchuck on the stairs, but I never mentioned it to anybody because whatever it meant, I didn't want to know.

The goose bumps came back while I was standing there. Was I really never going to see Zoe again? Was something going to happen to her? Was her spirit going to start floating around? Did spirits float around? Slip in and follow you through opened doors? I got the shivers, a spineful, and slowly, slowly looked over my shoulder.

The phone rang. I jumped and hit my hip against the counter and then stood, trying to get air back in my lungs. I felt like ripping the phone off the wall and stomping it to death.

"Hello?"

"Is Zoe there?" It was Sonny.

"What?"

"Zoe. Is she there?"

chapter

11

~ For half a second I pictured Zoe falling out of Sonny's car and Sonny not realizing it. Then it occurred to me. "Is this a joke?"

"She ran away from home," Sonny said.

"What do you mean? What are you talking about?"

"About fifteen minutes ago. We stopped by her house on the way to the doctor's. She took off on her bicycle."

"She ran away on her bicycle?"

"I started to chase her, but that just made her go faster. I was scared she'd crash."

I shook my head. "What're you— I don't understand. Why is she running away?"

Sonny didn't say anything.

"Hello?"

"Her mom and dad are here," Sonny said, stiffly.

"What? Her *mom?* Her mom is *there?*"

"Mm-hmm."

"What's her mom doing there?"

"If you see Zoe, could you call?"

"Did she bring her neurologist?"

"Her what?"

"Her boyfriend."

"Whose boyfriend?"

I pulled the phone away from my ear and glared at it. "Zoe's mom's. She's dating a neurologist."

"Not anymore."

"What do you mean?"

"I'll be over in a little bit."

"What does that mean, not anymore? What's her mom doing there?"

"Keep an eye out for Zoe, would you?"

"Just tell me why her mom came back."

"I'll see you."

"Oh, come on! Can you give me a *hint?*"

Pause. "Zoe."

"*Zoe?*"

" 'Bye."

Sonny hung up and I stood there blinking. *Zoe?* She was here for Zoe? What did that mean, that she was here for Zoe? Was she going to try to take her away? Kidnap her?

Have her live out in California with her and her neurologist? Why now? It'd been two years since she'd moved away. Why'd she come back now?

I started pacing between the sink and the table, checking the bay window every once in a while for Zoe. She wasn't supposed to be on her bike. That's what the doctor said. What if she rode into a tree? Fell over in an intersection? She might not have any identification on her. It might be days before we found out what happened. I checked my watch. What if she ran away and *got* away? Got a bunch of money at the bank and rode her bike to the airport and bought a ticket to Wichita. What if she just disappeared in Wichita? And I never saw her again?

The goose bumps crept back up my skin. I stuck my hands deep in my pockets and kept pacing. I should've talked to her, should've told her things. It sucks how you never know for sure if you're ever going to see someone again. Any day they could run away. Get hit by a car. Fly off to Australia. Become a rock star. Zoe could be gone forever. I didn't remember even saying good-bye.

I checked my watch again and tried taking a deep breath, then marched over to the broom closet and pulled out the ironing board. Mom always used to iron when she was worried. She probably didn't do any ironing anymore, now that she worked for the big law firm in Chicago, but when we were little and Dad was flying in a snowstorm or Tom was camping overnight with the Cub Scouts, Mom would get out the ironing board.

I went upstairs and grabbed the pile of ironing off the top shelf of my closet and brought it back down to the kitchen. There were shirts I'd forgotten I owned, and it felt a little like Christmas, finding all this stuff.

The saliva sizzled when I licked my finger and tapped it against the iron like Mom used to do. It seemed amazing to me that some things always worked exactly the same way.

I was pretty good at ironing—getting the cloth flat, running the iron across, wiping out the wrinkles, listening to the gasp of steam as I lifted the iron off. I felt like I could've done it for a living, if there was any money in it.

The phone rang. I quick took two giant steps, but it was only Matilda, calling from New York to tell me she and Dad got there OK.

"Your little sister is terrified about opening

night. Twice she told me she wished you were here to fight with so she could calm down."

I rolled my eyes.

"Say a prayer for her, would you, Haley?"

What was it with this prayer business? Since when were we this religious family? "Tell her good luck," I said, trying to be nice, trying to get back to the ironing. It just didn't seem real that Tracy was about to go onstage in front of five thousand people, that she was beginning a worldwide tour, that millions of people were listening to her music on the radio. It was hard to believe that Trace was *famous*. Nothing had changed. I was still scared about failing physics. I was still going to a flunky college buried in the tobacco fields of North Carolina. It just seemed like having a rock star in the family should change *everything*. I should be smarter. Better looking. I should be able to *relax*.

I saw Sonny's car pull up out front and quick got off the phone.

"What is going on?" I called out, walking across the front lawn. "What is her *mother* doing here?"

Sonny was standing on the other side of the car and looked at me surprised, like he didn't know I was going to be here.

"Did she just show up?" I was on the passenger's side, squinting from the sun shining low over the Abernathys' house across the street.

"Mr. Mudd called her," Sonny said, not looking at me.

"Why?"

Sonny shifted his weight and put a hand on the roof of the car.

"Why'd he call her?"

He looked like he had intestinal flu.

"Sonny?"

"It was about Zoe," he said.

"What about her?"

Sonny started to shake his head, and then looked down the street like he'd forgotten the question.

"What about her?"

"I can't tell you."

I lifted my hand and blocked the sun from my eyes. "Is she dying?"

Sonny just looked.

"Is she dying? If she's dying, just say it. Does she have some disease?"

"Did she tell you that?"

"Just— Could you answer the question? Is she dying from some weird disease?"

"No."

"Is she just dying?"

"She's not dying," Sonny said, shaking his head.

I put my hands on my hips. "Then—what. Is her father dying? Her *mother* dying?"

"No one's dying, that I know of."

"Then what's she going around crying about?"

Again with the intestinal problems.

"Is it just the boyfriend up in Delaware?"

Sonny looked at me, then tried to cover up. "You need to talk to her."

"It's the asshole boyfriend, isn't it."

"I really think you need to talk—"

"OK, OK, OK." I turned and headed back to the house. I was relieved she wasn't dying, but it pissed me off that she was broken-hearted over the jerk in Delaware. I walked into the kitchen and over to the sink and stood staring down into the drain, my hands braced against the edge of the counter like I was about to throw up. What is it about girls, that they go around liking assholes? What's the appeal? Is it sexy being a jerk?

Sonny knocked on the door, opened it, and stuck his head in. "What're you doing?"

"Brushing my teeth."

Sonny waited. "Can I call my house?"

"Supposedly if I was under hypnosis I'd understand what the hell is going on."

Sonny got his mom on the phone and asked if Zoe had called. I held my breath and listened.

"Anything?" I asked when Sonny got off the phone.

"No."

I shook my head. "Why didn't her folks just stop her?"

"They couldn't, really."

"Why not?"

"They didn't have any clothes on."

I turned around. "They were naked?"

"When we got there, they were upstairs making love."

I blinked. "How do you know?"

"We could hear them."

"From the first floor?"

"I don't think they were expecting us."

"You could hear them from the first floor?" I tried to imagine it. "How old are they?"

Sonny told me how Zoe was embarrassed and didn't know who her dad was up there with and hollered at them from the foot of the stairs. I was still trying to picture Mr. and Mrs. Mudd, still wondering how *parents* could go around being so loud having sex.

Sonny just kept talking. ". . . then the two of them appeared at the top of the stairs."

I looked at Sonny. *"Naked?"*

"They had sheets draped around them."

I exhaled fast. At least Zoe didn't have a mom and dad who walked around completely naked. "And Zoe just took off?"

"It might have been the surprise," Sonny said.

I pictured Zoe riding into the sunset on her bicycle.

"I think I might drive down to the mall and see if I can find her."

I shrugged and looked out the window at the weeds in Matilda's garden.

"Could she stay," Sonny asked, "if she came over here?"

I turned around. "What?"

"She might show up here."

My heart started going. "Why?"

"She knows where you live."

"Oh."

"Plus she thinks you've got integrity."

"Whatever *that* means." I still felt stupid about my heart taking off like that.

"So if she showed up here, would it be all right with you if she stayed overnight?"

"Sonny—" He was only making it worse.

"Look, just— She's not coming over here, so just—"

"She trusts you."

"Wonderful. OK? Just— Are you going to the mall?"

Sonny didn't move. "It's all right, then, if she stays?"

"Will you stop? She's not—" There was only one way to get rid of him. "Fine. Yes. Absolutely. She can stay forever. OK? Goodbye."

Sonny left. I looked back out the window. *Integrity.* Who cared about integrity? I wasn't running for office, for crying out loud. I didn't even *have* integrity. Why couldn't she have said something about a sense of humor? A nice smile, even? *Integrity.*

"Shit."

Matilda's garden looked pathetic. She hadn't touched it all spring because the pregnancy screwed up her balance. I'd seen her out there a couple of times, just looking, and I was going to offer to go out and pull weeds and stuff, but then Dad would piss me off or Matilda would be fixing Tracy's hair and I wouldn't get a chance to say anything.

Zoe had to get over the asshole boyfriend eventually. Maybe she and Sonny really would live together. Maybe they'd start going out. Maybe they'd keep going out and end up getting married and having kids. Sonny could sit them up on his lap and tell them about his first date with their mom, when he nearly got shot in the head and had this spiritual experience that changed his life.

I held on to the edge of the counter and stared down at the garbage disposal. It could all happen. It wasn't make-believe anymore. Sonny was eighteen. Zoe was almost eighteen. Things like getting married could happen now. Mom was eighteen when she and Dad got married. Sue Trainer and Brett Colson were getting married during beach week after graduation. That stuff could happen now.

I tried getting some air in my lungs, imagining going to Zoe and Sonny's wedding. It just seemed amazing to me that whole lives could start to happen. People making decisions that lasted forever. One day they're marking you tardy for walking in after the bell rings, the next day they're telling you to go do whatever the hell you want.

I went into the family room and turned on MTV. Sat there as the room got dark, watching beautiful women gyrate and grimace like they were going to collapse and die if someone didn't have sex with them soon. I realized I was going to have to learn how to drink beer before I went to Zoe and Sonny's wedding. I felt like I could be happy for them as long as I was pretty drunk.

I turned the TV off and went upstairs and read for a long while, trying to get sleepy. This whole wedding thing kept coming back over and over, and then on top of that I started thinking about physics. And math. And the stupid oral presentation in French that I was supposed to make two weeks ago.

I rolled over, stuffed the side of my head into my pillow. How many seniors in high school were there in the world still losing sleep over *homework?* People weren't thinking about homework. They were thinking about the prom. Beach week. Getting married. College. When was the last time I thought about college?

I got to sleep eventually but woke up again and again, until finally I looked out the window and saw deep blue instead of black. Morning. At last. The window was open and the room was damp and cold, like I was camping. I sat up in bed and wrapped a blanket around me and imagined going downstairs and making a cup of coffee. Sitting at the kitchen table, sipping it, taking my time. Maybe that had been my problem all along—I just didn't get up early enough.

I glanced over at the predawn blue outside, and a light caught my eye. I squinted. My car. The interior light was on in my car. I'd parked it under the big tree, so I couldn't see everything, but there was definitely a light on down there. Had I killed the battery?

Creeeaaak.

Holy shit. That was my door. Someone was down there. Someone was down there, opening my door. I flung the covers off me, knelt down by the window for a better look. All I could see was a body moving around, getting out of the car.

"Holy shit," I whispered. I wasn't thinking, should've dialed 911. Instead I went tearing down the stairs, threw the door open, and ran outside. Then stopped.

"Zoe?"

chapter

12

~ She was standing by the driver's-side door, the interior light shining on her. She looked up suddenly, like a deer hearing a shotgun.

"Hi," I said, trying to wave friendly in the dusky blue. Zoe quick shut the door. I walked slowly across the grass, freezing cold wet on my bare feet. I was naked except for gym shorts, and hugged my arms against my body. "You want a cup of coffee?" I asked, squinting again, trying to see Zoe in the dark under the tree. She was doing something. I could hear her doing something. "Some pancakes?" I was still walking slowly and heard a rolling sound. Bicycle wheels. Shit. "Zoe, wait a second."

She was on her bike now, past the tree. I could see her silhouette.

"Let me just make some pancakes," I called, and stood at the edge of the lawn, watching her pedal down the street. "You're not even supposed to be *on* your stupid bicycle."

I stood shivering, my feet feeling like they were getting frostbite, and looked over at the car. Under the tree was darker than the rest of the street, and I couldn't see anything. I went over to the driver's side and—*creeeaaak*—opened the door. A wisp of warmth drifted out. I climbed in, bracing myself for cold vinyl against my bare back, but instead the vinyl felt soft and warm. She'd been sitting here. I closed the door, not wanting to lose any of the heat, any of the smell. It was like something outside, the smell. Cut grass. Wet flowers. Something. Was it her perfume? Shampoo? Deodorant? I sat there, breathing. Down the street the sky was turning streaky with gray and pink. Everything felt big and mysterious, and I imagined this was what praying was like when you did it right. From the light coming in through the windshield I could see a blue plastic bag next to me on the seat. Inside was an open box of saltines, an empty ginger ale bottle, and a white-and-pink bag from Dunkin' Donuts. It felt like there was a doughnut still in the bag, and I reached in, pulled it out, and held it up to the windshield. Chocolate cream. I loved chocolate cream.

"Mmm," I said, taking a bite and looking down the street, wishing Zoe would come back for her doughnut. I licked my fingers. God, I loved chocolate cream. I felt like I could spend the rest of my life here, looking at the sky. All I needed was a fresh supply of doughnuts.

I went back inside and made coffee and sipped it at the kitchen table, my Dad's sheepskin coat draped over my shoulders like a cape. I was still wrapped up in the sky and the doughnut and the warm vinyl, and I decided I'd talk to Zoe at school. I'd done enough of not talking to her. Now I'd talk. Thank her for the doughnut. Tell her things. Take my time, pick the right words. Just talk.

I didn't feel as calm about it when I got to school and saw her bike chained to the bike rack and the hordes walking by me fast, everyone looking in a hurry to get somewhere and do something. I looked at my watch without meaning to and tried to take deep breaths to stop my heart from acting up. I didn't want to see her now, except maybe from a distance. I wasn't ready, yet, for talking—and I didn't want to mess it up—so I went straight to math and sat there, looking out at the trees, the branches perfectly still. Down below, two girls and a guy were sitting in a little circle on the grass. I watched them talk, watched them sprawl out, feeling a little like I'd wasted my four years of high school.

Mr. Wortman was putting problems up on the board. I got out my book and tried the homework, which was fine for the first eleven problems because my answers matched the ones in the back of the book. After that none of my answers matched, though, which meant I didn't really know what the hell I was doing. I tried working all the problems and kept hoping something would click, some step would come to me, but I just couldn't see it.

Sonny showed up late and sat down as the second bell rang. "Zoe's here," he said, out of breath.

"I know," I told him.

"Did you talk to her?"

"I saw her bike."

Mr. Wortman looked at the notes on his podium and announced he was checking homework. Shit. I quick got out a blank sheet of paper and copied my work for the first eleven problems. Mr. Wortman tried hard to explain stuff and took it personally when we didn't understand something. Halfway through the year I realized if I didn't understand something I was better off just telling him I didn't try it.

While I was copying the problems I looked over at Sonny. "Where's your homework?"

He was thinking about something else and it took him a second to realize what I'd said. "I didn't do it."

"You didn't do your homework?" I almost didn't believe him but then I noticed his hair was a mess and his skin looked like yogurt. "Are you sick?"

"I was looking for Zoe."

"All night?"

"A lot of it."

Was he madly in love with her? Was this going to be worse than Carey? Should I even tell him about Zoe spending the night in my car?

Before I could decide, the door opened and Mr. Urthwon, our principal, was standing there. Someone was in trouble. The only time we saw Mr. Urthwon in a classroom was when someone was in serious trouble. They brought a gun to school. They blew up some teacher's car. Counselors came if someone in the family died, and assistant principals dealt with all the small stuff—cutting class, smoking, calling a teacher an asshole. You had to really do something to get Mr. Urthwon.

He stood at the door and cleared his throat. He always cleared his throat before he said something; it seemed like a trick he'd learned in some class on public speaking. "Mr. Wortman," he said, clearing his throat again, "could I speak with Sonny Prendergast?"

My eyes spun around, but Sonny didn't look surprised. I watched him, stared at him as he collected his books and stood up without looking my way. What the hell was going on? Was it something with Zoe? Something about last night? Sonny said he spent all night looking for her. He hadn't done anything wrong. Sonny never did anything wrong. He—

I swallowed. Stared down at my desk. Maybe it was about the night before. The night at Carey's. Maybe there was an investigation. Now they were taking him in and charging him with trespassing.

Mr. Urthwon let Sonny walk ahead of him through the door, cleared his throat, thanked Mr. Wortman, and closed the door on his way out. People were whispering; it sounded like snakes in the closet.

Michelle Gordan, one of Carey Castle's field hockey buddies, turned and talked to me for the first time in my life. "What's going on?"

"What."

"With Sonny," she said, her brows crossed like I was some incompetent employee. "Is he in trouble?"

"It's the newspaper," I told her. "Some award thing."

She studied me. "You sure about that?"

"What. You think he robbed a bank?"

"I think you don't know what you're talking about." She turned back and arranged her pages of homework. I looked over at the door, and my heart started up. It had to be about the other night. What the hell else could it be? Sonny never did anything. Never missed homework, never ran a yellow light, never even slammed his locker.

What was Mr. Urthwon going to ask him? What would Sonny say? He was pathetically honest. He'd tell him everything. Put it in essay form, if he wanted.

I looked at Mr. Wortman shifty-eyed, and took a deep breath and started to cough. I tried a pukey cough at first, but it felt like I might tear a lung out, so I switched over to a simple dry cough that sounded almost like Mr. Urthwon clearing his throat.

Mr. Wortman turned and looked at me. I held up my hand and stopped for a second, like I was fighting to get it under control, but then started right back in again, louder, grabbing my throat and grimacing, straining to stop. Michelle turned back around and gave me a scornful look.

"Why don't you get some water?" Mr. Wortman suggested. Finally. I nodded and kept coughing on my way out and didn't stop until I turned the corner and headed fast for the main office.

I looked over my shoulder, checking for hall monitors. They were easier to spot now that the three of them had decided it would be cool to shave their heads. I wondered how the school decided to hire men who thought shaving their heads was a cool thing.

I glanced outside, walking by the doors at the main entrance, and almost stopped in my tracks. Oh, my God. My stomach got caught in an updraft as I stared at the police car illegally parked out in the fire lane. Oh, my God.

I got to the main office and stepped inside. It was freezing. Mr. Urthwon must have loved air-conditioning, because the place was always freezing. I walked by Miss Adams at the front desk without even looking at her, but back by the administrative offices Mrs. Chichester was sitting ramrod straight at her computer, wearing the same tan cardigan sweater she always wore. Even just sitting there typing, she seemed ready to attack, like one of those growling dogs guarding the gates of hell. I swallowed, thought about trying to just walk by her, but chickened out. I stopped and looked at the wall where there was the list of honor roll students. Everyone I knew was on it. Zoe. Sonny. Carey Castle. Michelle Gordan. The whole world was on the stupid honor roll.

Down past Mrs. Chichester, Mr. Urthwon's door was closed. Were the police in there? Interrogating Sonny? Did they read him his Miranda rights? Maybe we could get off on a technicality. I glanced at Mrs. Chichester, wondered if she ever took a coffee break, ever went to the bathroom.

"Can I help you?" she asked, still typing, still looking at her computer screen.

"Uh—" My heart started beating like a

fugitive's, and I realized I was shivering. "No, no, thanks. I was just—checking the honor roll."

Mrs. Chichester spun in her seat and looked at me, her nostrils flaring like an animal smelling blood. "You're Hale O'Reilly, aren't you?"

I turned. Had administrators been talking about me? Was I going to win one of the awards at graduation? "Well—yeah," I said, almost smiling.

"Tracy O'Reilly's brother?"

"Oh. Yeah." I felt like crawling under the carpet. *Graduation award.* How'd I think I was going to get an award? I wasn't even on the stupid honor roll.

Mrs. Chichester started telling me about her niece, who was a big Memento Mori fan and idolized Tracy. I kept nodding. Just what you want to hear about: people idolizing your little sister; people recognizing you because you're related to her. Maybe I could even write my autobiography someday. *Her Brother.*

"Does she give autographs?" Mrs. Chichester asked. I saw my chance and was all polite and told her I'd get one of those eight-by-ten glossies, get Tracy to sign it. Mrs. Chichester thanked me, then asked if I wasn't supposed to be in class. So much for kissing up.

Back out in the hallway I checked my watch. Mr. Urthwon couldn't keep Sonny in there forever, and I figured I'd just wait out here. I looked left down the hallway, then right. Saw a shiny bald head. Shit. Mr. Lebutkin, headed my way, talking into his walkie-talkie. The hall monitors loved their walkie-talkies; they acted like they were in a war zone, stuck behind enemy lines. If someone ever issued them guns, there'd be dead kids all over the place.

I ducked across the hall into Guidance, quick sat down in the waiting room, my back to the row of windows out to the hallway. I was dying to look back, see what Lebutkin was doing, but instead I kept my neck stiff and looked at the man and woman sitting across from me. The woman's red skirt was too short, so she had to keep her knees tightly crossed. I turned my head a little and bent my eyes all the way to one side, trying to see out the windows behind me. No Lebutkin.

"I want to know where she was," the woman said.

"Maggie." The man sounded tired.

"I want to know where she was, and I want to know who she was with."

"Can we just talk to her?"

"It's a little late for talk, don't you think?" The woman switched the leg she was crossing.

The man closed his eyes. They both looked disheveled, exhausted, like they'd been arguing for days, weeks. The woman's hair was a mess. I casually looked behind me at the hallway, which was empty. Where was Lebutkin?

"You should have talked to her a long time ago," the woman said.

"I was by myself," the man said, ready to collapse. "I did the best I could."

"Don't start, Harry. I begged her to come out and live with me."

"She didn't like the idea of you shacking up with a neurologist."

I turned, looked at the man, then the woman, then back at the man. Neurologist? Did he say neurologist?

Holy shit.

chapter

13

~ "Oh, *please*." The woman was practically spitting. "*Shacking up*. You sound like it's 1968. We weren't shacking up. We had a date. One date."

I looked away. I'd been staring and didn't want them to notice. I knew these people. I'd heard about them. He was a lawyer and worked seventy- and eighty-hour weeks trying to avoid thinking about life. She grew up rich and had an affair with a college art professor who told her she wasn't an artist. I knew more than I wanted to about these people sitting across from me. I knew that when they fought he wouldn't listen to her until she started to throw things. He was drunk at his father's funeral and cried. She loved the smell of coffee but went off the deep end when she had caffeine.

"That's not what you told her on the phone," Mr. Mudd said. "You didn't say anything about one date. You told her you were *seeing* him."

"*Seeing* him is not *living with* him."

I glanced up at them and jerked my eyes back to the carpet. I couldn't believe I didn't recognize her before. She looked just like Zoe, only with wrinkles. Her voice even boomed the same way.

"You told her you were seeing him," Mr. Mudd repeated. It must have been a lawyer trick; Mom used to repeat things all the time when she fought with Dad. "You were out there a week and were seeing this—this neurologist. She assumed you went out there to live with him."

Mrs. Mudd's whole body tensed, like she was bracing for a crash. "And I suppose it would have been impossible for you to tell her the *real* reason I left."

"Would you keep it down?" Mr. Mudd said, sounding disgusted and glancing over at me.

"Why didn't you tell her? Or why didn't you get Herr Fräulein to tell her?"

I glanced up.

Mr. Mudd caught me looking and wheeled toward Mrs. Mudd and spoke through his teeth. "Not here, Maggie."

"Don't *Maggie* me. I'm tired of being Maggie'd."

Mr. Mudd sagged like a dead man. "I told you what happened."

"That's right. Your secretary attacked you."

"That's not what I said."

"Held you at gunpoint and forced you take your clothes off."

"Maggie!" Mr. Mudd grunted, his voice straining like he was trying to hold up the end of a car.

The hallway door opened, and Mr. Lebutkin walked in. He was twenty-four or twenty-five but would've looked like a student without the shaved head. I rubbed my forehead like I had a splitting headache, hid my face. Mr. Lebutkin didn't like me since we'd had a scene in the cafeteria last fall, when he accused me of stealing an ice-cream sandwich I'd already paid for. No matter what I said to him now, he thought I was making fun of him.

"They have her, ma'am," Mr. Lebutkin said, sounding like a doctor reporting test results. "They'll be here any minute now."

Mrs. Mudd just sat there with her arms crossed. Mr. Mudd said thank you.

"I'll notify Mr. Reynolds." Mr. Lebutkin headed back toward Mr. Reynolds's office but saw me and stopped. "What're you doing here?" he asked, his voice deeper.

"Waiting for Ms. Abernathy."

"Where's your pass?"

"It's in on her desk," I said, my heart in a mudslide. "She said to wait. Out here."

Mr. Lebutkin's eyes narrowed, looking at me, but before he could accuse me of something the door opened again and Zoe walked in, followed by the other two hall monitors, Mr. Howe and Mr. Frizetti. They were both short and looked like they'd been kicked around in high school.

"What's *he* doing here?" Zoe asked, tossing her head at me.

"What's *who* doing here?" her mom asked back in the same angry voice.

Zoe looked at me. "Let me guess. You called them."

Mrs. Mudd looked at me, then Zoe. "What are you talking about?"

"Now they think you're a hero."

Mrs. Mudd looked at Mr. Mudd. "What is she talking about?"

"I have no idea," Mr. Mudd said, and looked at me. "Who are you?"

I shook my head, but Mr. Lebutkin answered for me. "Hale O'Reilly." He looked over his shoulder down the corridor toward Ms. Abernathy's office and scratched his thick, bald head.

"You're Hale?" Mr. Mudd asked. I looked at him but got distracted by Mr. Lebutkin lumbering back toward Ms. Abernathy's office. Shit.

"Are you her boyfriend?" Mrs. Mudd asked. I stared.

"Oh, Mother, *please,*" Zoe said, sounding embarrassed. Was that what she thought? I was an embarrassment?

"Zoe, I want to meet your boyfriend. I want to talk to him."

"There's nothing to discuss," Zoe told her.

"I see we have everyone together now!" Mr. Reynolds said, rushing out of his office, pushing back a wisp of thin hair and then pressing his hands together in front of him like they were greeting each other. "Thanks very much, fellas," he said, patting Mr. Frizetti on the back. He and Mr. Howe were hanging around like they expected someone to give them a tip. Mr. Reynolds smiled.

"Shall we go into my office? It's small but I think we can—"

"I'm fine right here, thank you." Zoe crossed her arms, not looking at anybody, her weight on one foot.

Mr. Reynolds scratched his cheek. "It'd be more private in my office, I think."

"I'm supposed to be taking a quiz," Zoe said, not moving.

"Zoe, grow up, would you please?"

"Oh yes, Mom. Right away, Mom. Whatever would make you happy, Mom."

Mr. Reynolds glanced over at me. There was probably a law against holding family conferences in front of strangers. He waved his skinny arms like he was directing traffic. "I really think we might be better—"

"Tell me, Mr. Reynolds"—Zoe turned to look at him—"what do you think of a woman who leaves her family for a neurologist?"

Mr. Mudd bit his lip. "Zo."

"Is that appropriate behavior for a loving mother?"

Mr. Mudd stood up. "That's enough."

"When you were growing up, Mr. Reynolds, did your mother ever abandon you?"

Mrs. Mudd looked tired. "Zoe, you're making an idiot out of yourself."

"I'm terribly sorry, Mom."

"Zoe," I said.

"I didn't mean to embarrass you, Mom."

"Zoe."

She turned on me. *"What?"*

I looked up at her standing there. "Maybe there's stuff you don't know."

Zoe put her hands on her hips. "Oh, well, Dr. O'Reilly, famous family therapist, by all means, please enlighten me."

Past Zoe I could see Ms. Abernathy waddling toward us, followed by Lebutkin.

"Hale?" she said, her voice soft, hurt. Ms. Abernathy is one of those young counselors who are sure that deep down inside every kid has a good heart. I acted like I didn't hear her.

"Are you coming home tonight?" Mrs. Mudd asked, looking down at the carpet, sounding defeated.

"No," Zoe said. "Are you?"

"Hale?" Ms. Abernathy called. She was short and fat and couldn't get around Zoe.

"We need to know where you're going to be," Mr. Mudd said.

"Around," Zoe said.

"With your boyfriend?" Mrs. Mudd asked.

"Will you let up about the boyfriend? There is no boyfriend."

Ms. Abernathy was too nice to push Zoe out of the way and bent over sideways, leaning around her, to look at me. "Hale, did you want to see me?"

"We need to know where you're going to be, Zoe."

"I have no idea."

Mr. Mudd kept his voice a cold monotone. "We were up all night. We were terrified."

"Daddy . . . I can take care of myself."

"We need to know where you're going to be."

"I'll be fine!"

"Hale, did you need something?" Ms. Abernathy asked, still bent over, smiling.

I kept acting like I didn't notice.

"Where are you going to be?" Mr. Mudd asked.

"Daddy!"

He was stone. "Where are you going to be?"

Zoe was speechless, then her lips went flat, angry, and she jabbed a finger at me. "His house."

Everyone looked at me.

"Who're you?" Mrs. Mudd asked.

"Her physics partner," Mr. Mudd said. I looked at him.

"We already worked it out," Zoe said, talking fast. "I can sleep in his sister's room. She's the famous one in the band. She likes chili."

"You're staying at a *boy's* house?"

"Is this all right with your parents?" Mr. Mudd asked.

"What." I nodded. "Yeah. Sure."

"Hale?" Ms. Abernathy bounced up on her toes, starting to sound a little pissed off. "Can I talk to you for a second?"

"It was nice meeting you," I said, holding out my hand to Mr. Mudd.

"You, too, Hale." He sounded sad, like he'd heard something about me. I gave Zoe a look as I followed Ms. Abernathy. She ushered me into her office, and I looked over my shoulder and saw Lebutkin loitering out in the hallway like he was waiting to beat the crap out of me.

"Sit, sit," Ms. Abernathy said, sitting down herself, her body spreading out and filling the whole chair. I sat down on the edge of my chair and looked at a picture of a white dog on her desk. Ms. Abernathy nodded, looking at me, and made a little church steeple with her fingers, tapping the top of the steeple against her lips.

"So how are things going?"

She'd obviously had training about how to get kids to open up.

"Zoe's mom came back yesterday. She'd been away for two years because she found out Zoe's dad was sleeping with his secretary."

Ms. Abernathy just kept nodding like she heard this kind of thing all the time. I told her about Zoe running away, and how she and her mom didn't talk because Zoe thought her mom was living with a neurologist. Ms. Abernathy touched pieces of paper on her desk like she was only half listening, but she kept pumping me for more details that I had to start making up until the bell rang for the end of first period and I could get out of there.

Mrs. Mudd and Mr. Reynolds were whispering to each other in the waiting room when I came back through. I glanced over at Mr. Reynolds's door, which was closed. Was Mr. Mudd in there with Zoe? Telling her about his Herr Fräulein? I thought about sticking around but glanced over at Mrs.

Mudd and saw her staring at me like this was all my fault.

I went back and got my books from math and then looked at my watch through French and government and psychology, waiting for lunch, waiting to talk to Sonny, to talk to Zoe. I needed to find out what was happening. What'd the police want with Sonny? Did Zoe really plan on staying over at my house? I couldn't believe all this stuff was going on, and I had to sit there listening to a review of Pavlov's dogs.

I got to the cafeteria early and waited in our usual spot, but no one showed up. Did they expel Sonny? Arrest him? Take him away? I got an asthma feeling, sitting there watching all these faces, bodies, voices going by. This was crazy, arresting Sonny. Did they have any idea what this guy was like? Did they know he carried spiders outside instead of squashing them? And where the hell was Zoe? She wouldn't have gone off with her folks. Did the police get her, too? Were all three of us getting arrested? I tried to swallow. Dad was going to kill me. If I got arrested and Willis College kicked me out before I even got there, Dad would never talk to me again. And Matilda would sit there in the kitchen with that basketball belly in front of her and stare down at the floor like a friend had died. Like I'd run them over, drunk driving.

My lungs felt dried up by the time I got to English. I kept expecting the knock on the door, kept expecting Mr. Urthwon to stick his head in and clear his throat. Toward the end of class I started wondering what they were waiting for. Were they trying to notify Dad before they actually picked me up? Were they calling up to New York, trying to talk to him?

Pong. Pong. Pong.

I walked slowly to physics. Please, God. Please let Zoe be there. I tried to get some air in my lungs and glanced in from the hallway.

No Zoe.

Shit.

A hand clamped down on my arm. Oh, God. Miranda rights. Remember Miranda rights, I told myself, turning my head and seeing Zoe.

"Quick, quick, quick," she said, pulling me away from the doorway. "I need your keys."

"What?"

"I need to borrow your car."

chapter

14

~ "What do you mean?" I asked, stalling.

"I need to go somewhere," Zoe said, making a quick circular motion with her hand, like I needed to start thinking faster.

"Where?"

"I'll tell you later."

"Are you running away?"

Zoe rolled her eyes. "Just give me the keys. Please?"

I was still suspicious, didn't want Zoe running away in my car. "Did your dad say anything—"

"I don't want to talk about it."

"I'm just wondering if he told you—"

"I—don't—want—to talk about it."

He'd told her. Zoe knew about the secretary. Would that make her run away? Was she mad enough at her dad to just take off? Or was she going to follow him in the car, waiting to run him over?

"I'm asking you—please."

"What about physics?"

"I'll be careful. I promise."

"You're just going to cut?"

Zoe blinked at me. "It's about Sonny."

I looked at her. I could count my heartbeats. "Did the police talk to you?"

Zoe shook her head. "Sonny talked to me."

"What do you mean? When?"

"At lunch. We went to Burger King."

"I thought— What about the police?"

"They couldn't arrest him because they couldn't prove it was us the other night at Carey's house."

My stomach tried to get away.

Zoe talked fast, like she was trying to win a contest. "But Sonny's made a hundred and forty-six phone calls over there since spring break, so if any of us say *hello* to her or even *look* at her funny, they're going to charge all three of us with harassment."

"Wait." My mind had stopped somewhere around "a hundred and forty-six," and then the words "charge" and "harrassment" piled on.

"We can talk about it later. Right now I need your keys."

"A hundred and—" I tried to add up how many days it'd been since spring, tried to figure out how many calls a day Sonny'd been making. I needed a calculator. "Wait a second."

"Look, Hale. Just give me the keys."

"But how do they know?"

"I'll meet you at the mall after school. I promise."

"How do they know it's him?"

"You can get a ride with Sonny. He knows where to meet."

"Zoe! How do they know it's Sonny calling? He told us he never says anything."

Zoe gave me a look and talked without breathing. "Mrs. Castle got freaked out over spring break because she got these phone calls where the person wouldn't say anything so she ordered a service from the phone company called caller ID that lets you know the number of the person calling before you even answer the phone."

I stared. "Shit."

"She and Carey have a *log* of the calls that have come from Sonny's house."

"Holy—"

"Now can I have the keys? Please?"

When Dad bought me the Buick he made me promise I'd never, never, never loan my car to anybody. "Why can't you just wait? I'll go with you."

"I can't wait, and you can't go with me. Look, Hale. Could you just trust me? For once."

I looked at Zoe. Knew I was going to regret this. Even as I reached into my pocket, even as I held out the keys, I knew I was going to regret this.

Zoe grabbed the keys and reached over and leaned her mouth in like she was going to kiss me on the cheek.

"Just—" I backed away, holding my hands in front of me.

Pong. Pong. Pong.

I was late for physics. Mr. Lindsey pointed it out to me as I walked in. He had a thing about people being late and constantly reminded us that when he graded tests, late people never got the benefit of the doubt.

Just what I needed before the final exam.

I sat down and tried to take notes but kept picturing Zoe out there somewhere, driving my car. Where the hell was she going? Something to do with Sonny, she said. Was she going to go talk to the police? Tell them it was all her fault? All my fault? Was she going to go yell at Mrs. Castle and get all three of us arrested? What was it she said they'd charge us with? I couldn't remember the stupid word, and I stopped listening to Mr. Lindsey and just stared out the window, trying to think of the word and imagining actually getting handcuffed by the police. God, wouldn't Dad love it if they got back from New York and found a note from the police taped on the door:

Your son is in jail. Please come down and post bail when you get a chance.

He'd be pissed off with the police until they told him about me harassing some innocent girl— That was the word! *Harassment.* God, it sounded awful. It sounded like I went around pinching her butt.

Sonny was waiting outside Mr. Lindsey's door at the end of class. I told him how Zoe had taken off and how we were supposed to meet her at the mall.

"She said you'd know where to meet."

"Mr. Ahm's Formal Wear. She's going to help me pick out my tuxedo for Friday night."

I nodded, checking my watch, glancing over my shoulder. I was too embarrassed to look at Sonny, knowing about the hundred and forty-six phone calls. It just seemed so *weird*. Every day we had math together, we ate breakfast together, lunch together, and I had no idea he was going around calling his ex-girlfriend three or four times a day. It was like he was a double agent. A cross-dresser. A naked old man in a trench coat. I thought we were friends.

Now I had no idea what to even talk about. We walked through the hallways and across the senior parking lot without saying a word. Sonny started whistling under his breath like it was just an ordinary day. Better than an ordinary day. It was like the police had told him he'd aced some big research project.

We got to his car, and I started worrying again about Zoe. "I don't even know how she drives," I told him, climbing in and slamming my door.

"She'll be careful," Sonny said, his voice calm, like a lake at sunset. I looked over at him. Was he mentally deficient? He spent the day getting interrogated by police, threatened with arrest, and told that his ex-girlfriend and her mom had a written record of the calls he'd placed to her house. What was his voice doing sounding all peaceful?

"How do you know she'll be careful? You've never even seen her drive."

Sonny looked both ways twice before pulling out of his parking place. "I just know," he said, coasting through the parking lot at three miles an hour, his eyes shifting from the road to the speedometer and back. He was going to run over somebody, trying to stay under the speed limit.

"Do you know where she's going?"

"It can't be far if she's going to meet us at the mall."

Sonny's tranquilizer voice was getting to me, and I reached down to turn on the radio. When I looked up he was smiling like he'd just remembered a great joke. I punched the radio off. "What."

"Life just seems full of connections."

I looked up at the roof of the car, then out the windshield.

"Most of the time we don't even pay attention. We're not even aware of the—depth of life. We only see flat surfaces."

Unless we go over to our ex-girlfriend's house and nearly get shot in the head and start sounding like we're on drugs all the time. I looked out my window and watched the houses go by, their lawns smooth and green. Just listening to Sonny, looking out the window, the world felt overwhelming—so many houses, so many people, so many dinner tables.

"I still think Carey has the potential to be a very spiritual person, if she gives herself a chance."

I didn't move. How could he think about her, how could he mention her *name?* Wasn't he embarrassed about his stupid hundred and forty-six phone calls?

"Maybe that's why her father drinks," Sonny said. "To give himself a chance to find that spiritual part of himself."

He was starting to sound like one of Mom's self-help books. "Yeah," I said. "Maybe alcoholics are just saints in disguise."

Sonny's eyes drifted around—trees, sky. He was usually a lot more careful driving; he was making me nervous. "Maybe they just *want* to be saints," he said.

I kept my eyes on the road. "You could say that about practically anybody."

Sonny turned toward me. "That's right," he announced, blinking like he'd just woken up and didn't know where he was. "That's exactly right. Everyone wants to be a saint."

I leaned against my door and pointed. "Red light."

When we got into the mall Sonny looked at the stores and gawked at the high ceilings like some Oklahoma farm boy visiting New York for the first time. I walked a little ahead of him and kept checking my watch. Had he been like this since Derrick took the shot at him? How could Zoe take it?

"You realize how lucky we are?" he asked me.

"Yeah. *Mmm-hmm.*" I was looking over at a fancy luggage store, wondering how a place like that stays in business.

"Our lives haven't rushed by."

"You can say that again."

"We haven't had to grow up."

I stuck my hands in my pockets. "You sound like my dad."

"Our lives are still just adolescent."

I rolled my eyes. That was great. *Just* adolescent. Like our lives didn't count; we were too young to matter. *Just* adolescent. It was like saying someone was *just* male. *Just* blond. *Just* normal.

We found the tuxedo place downstairs near Sears. Mr. Ahm measured Sonny and kept shaking his head because Zoe had called him from Burger King and had told him the tuxedo was for tomorrow.

"Tomorrow too soon," he kept saying, but

he gave Sonny a couple of tuxedos to go try on. Then he pulled out his tape and wanted to measure me. I shook my head, told him I didn't need a tuxedo, but he just nodded his head.

"Miss say you, too."

I couldn't get him to understand, and I just let him measure me. He was trying to hand me a couple of suits to try on when Zoe showed up. She looked ready to hit somebody and wouldn't look at me.

"What's wrong?" I asked.

"Where's Sonny?"

"He's in the back. Why? What'd he do?"

Her eyes still bounced around, then landed on me. "Guess who taught Carey's photography class."

"Her what?"

"The one she started all the way back in January."

I stood there. "What are you talking about?"

"They knew each other."

"Who?"

"They planned on going to Florida together."

"*Who?*"

Zoe glared. "Carey and Derrick."

chapter

15

～ For the last three years Derrick had been a teaching assistant for Saturday photography classes down at the Smithsonian. The first week of Carey's class, back in January, he'd shown her how to load film. The second week they'd eaten lunch together. Then they started talking on the phone. By February they couldn't wait the whole week to see each other and started having a clandestine rendezvous every Wednesday night in the biography stacks of the public library.

Meeting in Florida over spring break hadn't been a miracle; they'd secretly planned the whole thing, not even telling their best friends about it. They booked separate flights down and then, the first night, convinced both their sets of friends to eat at the same pizza place on the boardwalk at eight o'clock. The place was packed, and there was a half-hour wait, but they ended up getting seated at tables right next to each other, and Teddy Billings, one of Derrick's friends, started hitting on Michelle Gordan, a friend of Carey's. No one even noticed when Carey and Derrick started talking to each other.

No one ever suspected a thing. No one ever would've known if Sonny hadn't told Zoe at lunch how Carey would be depressed every Saturday when he'd pick her up at the Metro stop after her photography class. Zoe'd only been half listening, but later, walking to physics, something clicked. She thought she remembered Derrick telling her about a job he had at the Smithsonian. So she drove my car over to Echo Falls, tracked him down in a computer graphics class, and confronted him about it. He confessed everything.

"Why?" I glanced over at the door to Sonny's changing room and back at Zoe. She'd been filling me in while she waited for Sonny to get out. "Why would Derrick confess?" I would've denied everything. I always deny everything.

"Maybe he felt guilty."

"So all this time, were they—?" I waved my hand, but Zoe shook her head.

"He claims they didn't even hold hands until the night she broke it off with Sonny."

"How thoughtful."

"What is he doing in there?" Zoe couldn't take waiting anymore and went back to the dressing rooms and knocked on Sonny's door. I started to pace, picturing Carey and Derrick meeting every week at the library, sitting cross-legged on the floor, facing each other.

"You try on," Mr. Ahm called over to me, pointing to two tuxedos he had hanging behind the counter.

"Oh no, that's OK," I told him, smiling, but he kept nodding as he grabbed the suits and headed toward me. I didn't want to be there anyway. "I've got to go pick up something," I said, kind of laughing, trying to be polite. "Thanks for your help."

I walked out to the parking lot and sat on the hood of Sonny's car. It seemed crazy that Sonny was on the verge of getting arrested for his stupid phone calls, but there weren't any laws against Carey lying to everybody about Derrick. I wished it had happened to me instead of Sonny. Sonny wouldn't be vengeful.

Sonny wouldn't confront her in the cafeteria, in front of her friends. Sonny wouldn't write an editorial for the newspaper about lying, about people with the reputation of being incredibly nice who end up lying through their teeth. He wouldn't walk into Mr. Urthwon's office and tell him they can't give Carey the E. Kellogg Citizenship Award at graduation because she's a liar. A liar and a cheat.

I got mad about it all over again and jumped off the car and looked around the parking lot like I wanted to pick a fight. It would have been OK if people knew. It drove me up a wall, people thinking Carey was this sweet girl. If only we could distribute flyers to the entire student body. And the faculty. Someone needed to tell the stupid, idiotic faculty. They *loved* Carey. Mrs. Roberts always used Carey as her example of a student doing community service. Mrs. Thompson made me want to puke, telling us about Carey helping her after her hip operation. And Mr. Manning—it was like *he* was waiting for Carey to turn eighteen so he could propose to her. Morons, all of them. Idiots.

The sky was overcast, and the clouds felt close to the ground. I leaned my butt against the car with my arms crossed and stared at the mall. I imagined taking over the PA system at school during the morning announcements. I'd have maybe five seconds before someone wrenched the microphone away from me, so I'd have to keep it short, like a headline. CAREY CASTLE LIES TO WORLD ABOUT BOYFRIEND. Something like that. I was trying to think of the shortest, most damaging way of saying it when I saw Zoe and Sonny walking out of the mall.

Sonny looked like a prisoner of war. His head was leaning to one side as if his brain had shifted and now he had this unbalanced load. Why wasn't he pissed off? Why wasn't he jumping into his car and driving off like a maniac?

I couldn't look at him. Zoe walked up and handed me my keys while Sonny went around and climbed in on the driver's side.

"He hasn't said anything."

I watched the mall. It suddenly occurred to me that Zoe was going to get in the car and the two of them were going to go drive off somewhere and I was going to spend the night eating frozen lasagna and wondering where the hell they were and what the hell they were doing. "So where's my car?" I asked, just wanting to get this over with.

Zoe pointed and then glanced at me. "Would it really be OK if I stayed over at your house?"

I looked at her. Was this a joke?

"Maybe Sonny could stay over, too."

"Oh. Yeah." Now I got it. "Sure." I marched toward my car, not saying good-bye, not looking back. Were they going to expect me to supply sheets? Wash them in the morning?

Sonny drove over to where my car was parked and waited while I got the engine started. I followed them, watching the two of them talk. It was nonstop lips moving, with Sonny talking more than he had in the last six months combined. I hate not knowing what people are talking about, and on top of that it seemed like Sonny was trying to set some record for slow driving. By the time we got to my house I felt like screaming. And it didn't help matters any when I was unlocking the side door and Sonny asked if it'd be OK if he had some beer.

I looked over my shoulder. "I thought you didn't drink."

"It's not that I don't," he said, still using his peaceful, druggie voice. "It's just that I never have."

"But now you want to find that spiritual self."

Sonny smiled. "Maybe it would help."

"Whatever," I said, shoving the door open. I headed straight back to the family room to check for phone messages, then went upstairs and sat at my desk. I could hear them talking downstairs—no words, just voices. This was ridiculous. This was *my* stupid house; I shouldn't have had to hide in my room. I clomped back down the stairs, making lots of noise so they knew I was coming. The first things I saw, walking into the kitchen, were the two beer cans on the kitchen table. At first I thought they'd both decided to start drinking, but then I saw Zoe with a glass of water and realized Sonny was just drinking fast.

I went around tidying the kitchen, putting glasses in the dishwasher and wiping down the counters even though they didn't need it. The conversation at the table had dried up. When I was upstairs they sounded like long-lost friends. Now all of a sudden they had nothing to talk about.

"What kind of pizza do you want?" Zoe asked. "I'm buying."

"Sausage and pepperoni," I said, fast, like I'd totally forgotten Sonny was a vegetarian.

I went back to the family room and clicked on the TV and sat on the floor in front of the couch. I could hear Zoe on the phone, ordering pizzas, and then the two of them started talking again in the kitchen. Zoe laughed like she was drunk. I found the local weather station and cranked up the elevator music they play in the background. According to the radar screen there was crap all over the place, but looking out the sliding glass door I couldn't see anything. I wouldn't have minded getting sucked up by a tornado and thrown down miles away. I'd heard about that kind of thing, knew it was possible.

Bing-bong.

I stood up, but Zoe got to the door first. It was the pizzas, delivered by an old man who kept apologizing like he thought Zoe was going to get him fired. Old delivery people depress me, and I couldn't take even looking at this guy, the way he kept bowing to Zoe like he was Quasimodo.

Sonny was opening another beer when I walked into the kitchen to set the table.

"How's the beer?" I asked, loudly pulling plates out of the cupboard.

"I don't feel that much different," Sonny said, talking louder than usual. "My joints work better, I think. I could go running and enjoy it."

Zoe'd gotten two pizzas—one vegetarian and one sausage and pepperoni. She took slices from the vegetarian pizza and made me feel guilty for having a whole pizza to myself. I stuffed my face, let them do the talking. They didn't say anything for a while, and then all they could talk about were the stupid pizza toppings. Crisp peppers, soggy mushrooms, onions just right. They sounded like kids talking when they know an adult's listening to them.

"I'm going to watch some TV," I said, taking pity on them. I grabbed another slice and headed back to the playroom and watched reruns of sitcoms that weren't funny the first time around. Outside it got dark. In the kitchen Sonny was laughing out loud. I heard him announce to Zoe that he was going to the bathroom, and I stared at the TV, listening for the bathroom door to shut. I grabbed my plate and took it back to the kitchen. Zoe was sitting there staring out the bay window at the dark street. I stopped as I walked in, quiet, just looking at her, but she saw my reflection in the window and turned.

"What is going on?" she whispered, angry.

I froze. "What."

"I thought he was your friend."

Terror struck my heart. Was it so obvious, the way I was looking at her? "I was just standing here."

"You couldn't even finish dinner with us?"

I blinked. "What?"

"You can't even stay in the same room?"

I didn't move. I thought she was mad at the way I was looking at her, at the way I felt about her when I was supposed to be Sonny's friend. But she hadn't noticed a thing, had no idea.

"Sonny thinks you're mad at him," she told me.

"For what?"

"How should I know?"

I threw my hands up and went back into the family room, the TV shining out into the dark like a beacon. God. I thought she'd noticed, thought she'd seen the way I was staring at her, thought she'd finally realized.

Sonny flushed and went back to the kitchen, and I slipped into the bathroom and shut the door. I could hear Zoe laugh again—another loud, annoying guffaw. I tried taking a deep breath, staring at myself in the mirror. I could handle this. I was sober, reasonable. I could deal with Zoe and Sonny being a thing. I inhaled and held my breath like I was diving underwater, opened the bathroom door, and headed back to the kitchen. When I walked through the doorway, Zoe was doubled over, laughing so hard she looked like she was going to cough up a liver. Sonny was slapping the table.

"He does a great Derrick impersonation," Zoe said, pointing at Sonny. "You've got to hear it."

I walked over to the sink, looking at the beer cans on the table. I'd never, ever heard Sonny do an impersonation of anybody. How'd he get to be so good at it? Did he practice at home with a tape recorder? I opened the dishwasher, dumped in the plates from dinner. I could see the reflection in the window of the two of them sitting practically in each other's laps over at the kitchen table.

"We think Derrick's going to go into politics," Zoe said.

"Congressman Krutz," Sonny said.

"Senator Krutz."

"*President Krutz!*" Sonny screamed, like it was the best joke he'd ever heard. I was closing the dishwasher and had to stop for a second. Since when did Sonny scream?

"There's sheets and stuff up in the closet at the top of the stairs," I said.

Zoe chopped off her laugh and looked at the clock radio on top of the refrigerator. "You're going to *bed?*"

"It's not— I'm just really tired," I said, trying to sound just really tired. "Let me know if you guys need anything. Good night." I went upstairs and closed my door.

It didn't make sense why the laughing was getting to me. What'd I expect Zoe to do? Help Sonny mope? Help him go burn down Carey's house? It was good she had him laughing, had him screaming out. I would've thought she was doing great if they'd been someplace else, if I didn't have to listen to it.

I walked over and sat at my desk and rubbed my eyes, thinking about Mr. and Mrs. Mudd, thinking about Sonny saying he could hear them from the first floor. Would Zoe be loud like that? Was it a genetic thing? If she and Sonny decided to have sex down there, was I going to hear them? I didn't care if they were having sex down there if I didn't have to *know* they were having sex down there. But if they made a ruckus, if I could hear them . . .

I climbed onto the bed and lay there with my hands behind my head, staring at the ceiling. I felt like a land mine with a hair trigger—one gasp from downstairs, one moan, one grunt, one *oooh,* one *ah,* and I'd explode.

Take the whole house down with me. What was I so mad about? People were having sex all over the place, and I wasn't mad at them. I wasn't going around the neighborhood screaming at people to stop having sex. It was a good thing, Sonny having sex. Sonny needed some sex. It'd probably be the best thing for him. Sex therapy.

Criiick.

I turned my head. Someone was on the stairs, taking the steps softly. Zoe. Sonny walked like he had lead feet, so it had to be Zoe on the stairs, coming up to get sheets and stuff. Here we go. I shut my eyes. Maybe if I brought my boom box over to the side of my bed and turned it up loud, maybe I could drown them out. Or maybe I should just leave and get a motel room.

Kunk. Kunk. Kunk.

I turned again. Was that my door? Was she knocking on my door?

"Hello?"

The door opened slowly, just enough for Zoe to stick her head in sideways. "Hi," she whispered.

Oh, my God.

I sat up and got off the bed and stood there beside it with my hands in my pockets.

Oh, my God.

chapter

16

~ "Do you have a big T-shirt I could wear?"

"I don't know," I said. I couldn't think, looked down at my feet.

Zoe opened the door farther and stepped inside, carrying a big white towel she must've gotten out of the linen closet. "I haven't taken a shower since yesterday morning and I feel yucky."

"OK," I said, bouncing my head in a nod and not looking at her as I marched over to my dresser. Zoe watched as I opened and closed drawers.

"Are you mad at me?"

"Here's something." It was a baggy

gray T-shirt that I used to wear a lot. "Is this OK?"

Zoe took the shirt. "Don't be mad at me."

"What. I'm not—" I could feel her looking at me. "Zoe, I'm not mad at you, OK?"

"Why won't you look at me?"

"Here, I'm looking at you. OK? Now would you just— The bathroom's over there."

Zoe kept staring but then left, finally. I closed the door and stood bent over, trying to force air into my lungs. Across the hall Zoe turned on the shower. I could hear the water and walked over and knelt by the window for some air. I pictured her first leg stepping into the tub, pictured drops of water landing on it, rolling down. Pictured the leg going all the way up to her body. God. I jumped up and went over to my desk, looking for something to do. I pushed some papers out of the way, checking to see what was underneath. This was ridiculous. What was wrong with me? So Zoe was across the hall taking a shower. So she was naked. So water was cascading down her naked body.

I grabbed a fistful of hair on top of my head. On a scale of one to ten, how sexually deviant was I? I yanked off clothes, got into my gym shorts, turned off all the lights, and got into bed.

One thousand.

Nine hundred ninety-nine.

Nine hundred ninety-eight.

Nine hundred ninety-seven.

How far would I get before I actually got to sleep?

Nine hundred ninety-six.

Nine hundred ninety-five.

Nine hundred ninety-four.

Nine hundred ninety-three.

Did this ever work? Did it ever put you to sleep? Or would you just get down into the six hundreds and start getting really depressed because you were never going to get to sleep? I lay there in the dark with my arms crossed. The shower water was still going, and I pictured Zoe in there, her hair wet, her face turned up into the spray of water, her shoulders naked and soapy, everything naked and soapy.

Shit. I reached back and grabbed my pillow and stuffed it on my head, wrapped it, and pulled it down over both ears. Even without hearing the water, though, she was there. That's the way it is with your imagination— you can't turn the stupid thing off. I closed my eyes and started humming a Mozart piano thing my dad played all the time. It had all these notes, so it was impossible to hum, which made it a good distraction.

Until the light went on.

My eyes shot open like you see in movies when people wake up from a terrible nightmare. Zoe was standing over at the door, wearing the gray T-shirt, just the gray T-shirt, and rubbing her hair with the white towel.

"Are you feeling OK?" she asked, her voice coming muffled through the pillow. She wasn't wearing a bra. I let go of the pillow and turned my eyes away. I couldn't look at her.

"Fine. Yeah. I was just humming." I sat up, draping the sheet over my shoulders and looking over at the window. "You find everything OK?" I asked, trying to sound conversational.

Zoe walked over and sat down on a corner of the bed. I pulled my legs all the way up and sat Indian style. "Nothing feels better than clean hair," she said.

To the window: "Yeah."

"Sonny's asleep."

I nodded. "He doesn't drink."

Zoe watched me watch the window. "What are you looking at?"

"What. Fireflies."

She kept rubbing the towel into her hair. "Do you want me to leave?"

My heart felt like a cannonball. "No."

"Do you want to talk?"

"Sure."

"Are you going to look at me?"

I looked at her, at her face. If I'd known where Tracy kept her bras, I would've gone and gotten Zoe one. She kept looking back at me until I couldn't take it anymore and turned back to the window. "How many beers did Sonny have?"

"He'll be OK."

"Are you going to . . ." I held my breath. ". . . sleep down there somewhere?"

"You mean with Sonny?"

"Not—I wasn't—I didn't—I guess, yeah."

"Sonny and I aren't sleeping together."

"Oh." I tried to swallow some air, my eyes still on the black window.

"I'm not that kind of girl," Zoe said, her voice shaky, like a little kid nervous about making a speech. When I looked over, her eyes were closed.

"Wait, wait, wait. Zoe—"

"I'm really not," she said, her chin quivering, her eyes squeezed tight, the tears coming anyway.

"Don't. Don't." I couldn't deal with her

crying. "I wasn't—I just—" I slid down the bed toward her, still holding the sheet up by my neck with my right hand. I started to put my left arm around her but stopped. "Zoe, I wouldn't—" Again with the arm, again I stopped. "I like you."

She nodded, her whole face pressed tight, the tears still falling.

"A lot," I said.

"I know." Zoe's body began to fall toward me, her face landing softly on my shoulder. I put my left arm around her, then my right. I pressed my hands against her back, felt her shake with sobs. The warmth of her body came through the thin T-shirt; her hands felt hot on my bare back. She sniffled a couple of times and nestled her head against the crook of my neck.

"You OK?"

Zoe didn't say anything, then spoke in her regular voice. "Do you have any clothes on?"

"Yeah. Yeah." I let go of her, scooted away, reaching for the sheet and getting it back up in front of me. "Gym shorts. I'm wearing gym shorts. Navy blue."

Zoe nodded and sniffled. I looked back out the window. So did Zoe. We both looked out the open window for a long time until finally Zoe sighed.

"Sonny called Carey."

I turned. "What?"

"He wanted to ask her why she did it, but there was no answer."

"Just now? He called from here?"

Zoe nodded.

"You let him?"

"I was in the bathroom."

"What—is he stupid?"

"He said if he'd been sober enough to drive, he would have gone over in person."

"If he'd been sober enough to drive, he wouldn't have been drunk enough to be so stupid." I pictured him making the call, punching the numbers in on the phone and sipping his beer. "They're going to arrest him. They're going to put him in jail. They might put all three of us in jail."

Zoe spoke softly, absently. "There are worse things."

I just looked, blinking. "I get arrested, I don't go to college."

She stared out the window. "There are worse things."

"Like what? Like dying? Like getting shot in the head in your ex-girlfriend's backyard? Is that what you're talking about? Great. Yeah. We're all alive. Terrific."

Zoe didn't say anything; she just slowly lay

down along the edge of the bed, facing the window. I got out of the way and just stared at her like she was bleeding to death.

"What's wrong?"

She rested her head down on her two hands and curled her legs up. "Is it cold in here?" She sounded practically asleep.

I wasn't sure what to do. I pulled the sheet up and spread it out over her, then reached down and got the blanket and did the same thing.

"Thanks," she said, grabbing the edge of the blanket and pulling it up under her chin.

I sat there, not moving, biting my lip. "Are you sick?"

Zoe shook her head, still facing away from me, toward the window.

"Why do you cry all the time?"

"Because."

I spoke softly, didn't want to get her going again. "Because what?"

"Because I'm . . ." She didn't move. I held my breath. ". . . different."

I looked at her cheek, at the clean, wet hair curled around behind her ear. "What does that mean?"

"Could we not talk about it?" Zoe asked in a twilight sleepy voice. "Just for tonight?"

I watched her. She looked pathetic, like an

orphan, with her head nestled against her two little hands. "Here." I leaned over and put my pillow at the top of her head, and Zoe reached up and pulled it under.

"Do you think you could turn out the light?" she asked in the same dreamy voice.

I sat there, feeling out of breath. What was she telling me? Turn out the light and what? Turn out the light and close the door on your way out? I climbed off the bed and walked over to the door. I stood there for a second, facing the switch, then reached up and hit it off. It was amazing how dark it got. I couldn't see anything, not even a shadow of a light coming from somewhere downstairs. I felt my way through the doorway but then stopped. "Did you— Do you want me to leave?"

From somewhere out there in the darkness: "No."

I tried to swallow. I looked down at the floor, even though I couldn't see it, and slid my feet back toward the bed. It was my room, I should've known how to get around, but I didn't want to walk on some sneaker out there and twist an ankle and fall down and wake Zoe up. Completely awake, she might not think this was such a great idea; she might start worrying I was going to assume something. I felt a little naked in my gym shorts and thought about trying to find some pajamas but then just shook my head at myself. We were sharing a bed, not a phone booth; there was plenty of room. As long as I stayed on my side, she didn't even have to know I was there.

The sheets were freezing on my legs as I climbed in under the covers. I reached down to the floor and felt around and found a couple of T-shirts and was rolling them up into each other when I heard Zoe moving around. I froze and listened.

"Where are you?"

I didn't move. If she wanted me sleeping on the floor, why didn't she say something? "Here," I said, defensive.

"What are you doing?"

I was leaning sideways on my elbow, facing my side of the bed. "I'm trying to make a pillow."

"Turn over for a second."

My eyes looked around in the dark.

"This way."

"What." I turned over and faced Zoe, leaning on my other elbow.

"Let me see your hand for a second."

"What?"

"Just give me your hand."

"What for?"

"I don't believe this," Zoe said, and poked at me.

"What—"

Her hand found my arm, then my fingers.

"Zoe—"

She turned back away from me, still holding my hand, and lay down, pressing my hand against her stomach. I was leaning on my other hand now so my arm could make it all the way over her. "Do you always sleep sitting up?" she asked.

I took a deep breath, sweating, and lay down half on my stomach, like I was reaching across the bed to set my alarm. I was trying to avoid brushing up against Zoe, didn't want her thinking I was jumping to any conclusions.

"You comfortable?"

"What. Yeah."

Zoe shimmied her body toward me. I quick moved the bottom half of my body away. Zoe kept moving until her back was against my chest, her hair in my face. "Good night."

I almost laughed. She actually thought I was going to sleep like this? She actually thought I was going to trust my body to not notice this girl in my bed? My body had already caught on. There was no way I could just go to sleep and leave it here. I opened my eyes, leaned my head back, trying to find my T-shirt pillow. Did I leave it on the floor? It didn't matter. My arm and shoulder were too twisted out of shape to worry about not having a pillow. And I didn't care. My eyes had adjusted to the dark and I could see the silhouette of Zoe's hair there in front of me. I got goose bumps, wanted to talk to her. About anything, I didn't care, as long as we could lie here in the dark with my hand against her stomach. God. A chill ran down my spine, and I closed my eyes and felt Zoe breathing against my arm. Was she asleep? I couldn't tell one way or another and almost whispered something, a secret, but then felt her hand let go of mine, like someone in a movie when they die. Was she dreaming? Was she drooling? Drooling on my pillow? I kept my eyes closed and felt my hand still against hers, warm, felt strands of her hair against my face. I leaned forward and gently kissed her hair and quietly listened to her body breathe.

chapter

17

～ It was dark and cold when I woke up. I lay there for a while feeling the chill on my face, outside the covers, feeling the warmth coming from Zoe, inside. I couldn't remember actually getting to sleep and for a long time I lay there trying to piece together what happened. Usually when I was awake it was easier to sort out the real parts from the dreams. I held my breath, listening to Zoe breathe. Her back was still to me and I wanted to slip my arms around her and snuggle up against her again, but I couldn't see anything and didn't want my hand landing on something and Zoe thinking I was trying to do something while she was asleep. I rolled over on my side and looked at her dark head on my pillow. I couldn't see much, and I was having a hard time remembering what she looked like, but I could still hear her voice, sleepy, whispering.

Outside the open window the air wasn't completely black but the deep blue that started morning. My stomach locked up— morning. Already. The night was gone. It never let up. Night. Day. Night. Day. A constant steady flow, no breaks. I should've stayed up, couldn't believe I'd slept through practically the whole thing. I'd wasted the whole night. *Sleeping.*

I sat up in the dark, my arms folded against the cold, my eyes feeling puffy from getting up this early. The idea of hot coffee seemed like something from a magic kingdom, and eventually I got up and went downstairs. Sonny was breathing asthmatically back in the family room, and I shut both doors to the kitchen before I turned on a light. I wanted Sonny to sleep, wanted Zoe to sleep. I just wanted to have some coffee by myself, and I stood there waiting, watching the coffee drip.

It was going a drop at a time and taking forever, and I started opening cupboards, just to distract myself. A box of pancake mix caught my eye. Pancakes. I could make

pancakes. I hadn't made them since maybe
the fourth grade, and back then Mom had
showed me how to do everything. I got the
box down and read the directions. Did we
have any eggs? I checked the refrigerator and
came back with eggs, milk, margarine; got
out the electric griddle. I was shivering now
and looked over and saw the coffee was
ready. I got the griddle going, mixed up some
batter, poured some coffee, topped it off with
some milk, and stood there with my hands
wrapped around my coffee mug, slurping sips
while the griddle heated up. The coffee was
delicious, and I suddenly got a goose-bumpy
feeling that life was going to be OK, that
there were doughnuts and pancakes and coffee and moments like this that were cold and
clear and just involved things that smelled
good.

The margarine sizzled when I flicked it
onto the griddle, and as soon as the batter
landed the smell of pancakes filled the room.
I'd forgotten how much I loved pancakes,
and my mouth watered as I stood there with
the spatula in one hand and my coffee mug
in the other. I ate half of the first batch right
off the griddle but then stopped because I
wanted to stockpile a bunch for Zoe. She'd
inhaled them the other night at the diner, and

I quick ladled out another griddleful, poured myself more coffee, and stared out the window over the sink at the backyard. The sky had gone light but still hadn't added color to anything.

A door creaked open. I looked over my shoulder.

"Hi," I whispered, turning back to the griddle, feeling shy. Zoe was wearing the bathrobe I'd left for her just outside the door to my room. "You like pancakes?" I asked.

"Uuuuuuugh."

I quick looked back over my shoulder. Zoe looked post-pukey white and walked slow and flatfooted like she'd swallowed a bomb. "You OK?"

"No." She waved a hand to shut me up, her eyes closing to slits. I didn't get it. She hadn't had anything to drink.

"Is it stomach flu?"

She waved her hand again, desperate. I didn't want her puking all over the kitchen floor and kept my mouth shut. I turned around and slid the spatula under the edges of the pancakes. Was this why she wasn't supposed to be riding her bicycle? Something to do with her balance? Her inner ear?

Zoe slowly walked over and stood behind me.

"You want some Alka-Seltzer?" I whispered, not making any sudden movements.

Zoe dropped her head down and pushed the top of her head into the middle of my back. For a long time I didn't hear anything, wasn't sure what I was supposed to do. The pancakes were getting the holes on top that meant they were ready to turn.

"I'm sorry," Zoe said.

"What."

Zoe pushed her head harder against me. "Last night never should have happened."

My eyes looked at the spatula, the pancakes, the edge of the griddle, the countertop, the wall outlet, the handle on the cupboard in front of me. "What—?" I stopped, decided I didn't want to know.

"I'm sorry," Zoe said. Again.

I reached over and turned off the griddle.

Zoe pressed her head harder into my back. "It's not what you think."

I nodded, carefully placed the spatula on the counter.

"It's hard to explain. I should have said something."

Zoe's head was still pressed against me, and I arched my back and slowly moved sideways.

"Hale," she said, feeling me move. "I just wanted it to be normal."

"Sure."

"It was nice."

She should've just stabbed me. "Don't—"

"I wasn't out to hurt you."

I was already headed toward the front hall and rattled my head furiously without looking back. "You— Don't worry."

"Hale."

I was on the stairs. Got up to the bathroom, got the water running, locked the door. *It's not what you think.* I shook my head. *It's not what you think.*

"What the hell do I think?" I had no idea what to think, had no idea what was going on. She was telling me last night was a *mistake?* What did she think was the mistake? Where was the mistake? I paced to the toilet and back, stared at the door. "Nothing happened! What do you think happened? Nothing!" Our bodies might've brushed up against each other in our sleep. Was she calling that a *mistake?* Was she holding us responsible for what happened to our bodies in our *sleep?*

I climbed into the shower, started shampooing my hair, practically pulling out clumps. She was crazy. She was out of her mind. "Tell me the mistake. Tell me what I'm *thinking*. You're telling me it's not what I'm thinking; tell me what I'm thinking." I wanted a baseball bat. Wanted to beat the shit out of the bathroom. Knock the sink off the wall. I was calmer back in my room getting dressed, stopped talking to myself. What the hell. I looked at myself in the mirror over my dresser.

"What. The. Hell."

Zoe was sitting against the front door as I came down the stairs. She had an arm around her stomach and a hand against the side of her face. She looked like a war victim. "Listen," she said. "I want to tell you something. It's important."

"Yeah." I turned the corner and walked through the kitchen.

"Hale—"

I slammed the door behind me, walked hard down the driveway, ready to run if I heard a door open. If she had something important to tell me, let her send a telegram. I drove to school with music turned up to jet-engine volume. *I'm sorry.* How many times did she say it? *I'm sorry. I'm sorry.* What was there to be sorry about? Nothing happened.

I stopped at Burger King and bought a large coffee and sat there blowing steam off the top of the cup. I looked out the window at the trees, the leaves already dark green like summer. What did it matter what she said? It didn't matter. She could be sorry all she wanted. In a week I'd never see her again.

I sat there for a long time and went back and got a refill on the coffee and an egg sandwich to soak up the caffeine. *A mistake.* That was what got to me, her calling last night a mistake. Why couldn't she just say she didn't want to see me anymore, or she was in love with Sonny, or *something?* Why'd she have to pick on last night?

I checked my watch. The warning bell for first period would've rung by now. I was safe showing up. If I skipped lunch and cut physics, I might get away with never seeing her. I drove to school and had to park in the service lane by the tennis courts. God, I hoped I was right about the parking tickets.

Last day of classes. It hit me, walking toward the main entrance. I couldn't believe it. The last day of high school. The last day of high school, and Zoe had to go and spoil it. I shook my head and looked up. Stopped.

"Holy shit."

Cop car. Parked in the No Standing zone.

I knew why they were here. Knew who they wanted to see, knew what was going on.

I started to walk again, faster, but then saw the doors to the main entrance opening and saw Sonny and an old cop and a young cop and Mr. Lebutkin all walking out. Oh, my God. Oh, my God. My stomach acted like I was about to impale myself on a meat hook. Shit. I swallowed, and started running.

"Excuse me. Excuse me, officer?" Was that what they liked being called? Officer? Was there something better? Your Honor? Your Majesty? "Excuse me." I was nearly in front of them now. "Sirs? Sirs?"

The old cop looked up. The young one seemed deaf.

"Stay out of this, O'Reilly," Mr. Lebutkin told me, following behind the three of them.

"Did Sonny tell you what happened?" I asked the old cop, backpedaling sideways as they came toward me. The old cop's eyes sagged like he'd done too many night shifts. "Did he explain what was going on?"

"O'Reilly, I'm warning you," Lebutkin called out. I wondered what the cops thought of his shaved head.

"Hale," Sonny said, shaking his head.

I pointed at Sonny, my heart hammering. "He found out yesterday that she cheated on him. OK?"

"She didn't cheat," Sonny said, like we'd

gone over this before. His hair was a mess.

"She lied to him. For two months she lied."

"This is your last warning, O'Reilly."

We were at the cop car now. The young cop had the back door open and was pushing Sonny in without even warning him to watch his head. I looked at the old cop.

"She told everybody she met this Derrick guy down in Florida, but she'd actually met him up here two months before. When she was still going out with Sonny. For two months she was seeing this guy and still going out with Sonny. Ask her."

"That's it! That's all she wrote." Lebutkin's hand shot out and grabbed onto my arm and quick had it twisted around my back like you see cops doing to the bad guy before they smush his face against a brick wall.

The young cop slammed the door closed but Sonny's window was rolled halfway down.

"It's going to be OK," he said, looking out at me, almost smiling. Was he smiling? He looked like a moron, a crazy.

"Sonny—" I shook my head.

He stared at me. "There are worse things."

"So what? That's not—"

Lebutkin pulled up harder on my arm. I

didn't think it was legal for him to be tearing my arm out of its socket, but the cops didn't seem to be noticing.

"Just ask her," I said to the older cop as he got in.

Lebutkin held my arm behind my back as the young cop started the car.

"I think you can let go now."

"Oh yeah?"

What a comeback. I stuck my other hand in my pocket and looked up at the sky like I was waiting for a bus. "I have Mr. Wortman first period. Room A-Thirty-eight."

Lebutkin laughed like he was sneezing. "Not today you don't."

I looked at him.

chapter

18

～ "I don't get a phone call?"

Lebutkin pointed. "Sit down."

"You ever hear of Miranda rights?"

"Sit down and shut up."

I'd never done in-school suspension, had never seen Mr. Lebutkin's room. It was the size of a walk-in closet and had seven desks crowded into two rows, the first row lined up against the front wall, the second row backed up to the back wall. I was the only customer today, and Lebutkin pointed to the first seat in the first row. I felt instantly claustrophobic, sitting there with this wall in my face. All along the front wall Lebutkin had taped up poster board with rules handwritten with a thick Magic Marker:

NO TALKING
NO EATING
NO DRINKING
NO HEADS ON DESKS
NO STANDING
NO LAUGHING
NO KiDDING

"Mind if I smoke?" I asked, staring ahead at the wall. Lebutkin was sitting in the back corner by the door in this tilting, executive-looking chair that I hoped the school didn't pay for. I could hear him leafing through magazines he'd probably stolen from the library.

"Mind if I sell some drugs?"

"Keep it up," Lebutkin told me.

I pulled a book out of my backpack, but it was impossible to concentrate with these stupid rules about to fall down on top of me. Lebutkin had done a sloppy job printing the letters, and the lowercase *i* in KiDDING was driving me crazy. It would've been so easy to fix. Was he just oblivious?

I looked at my watch, looked over my shoulder at Lebutkin. "I've got to make a presentation in French in twenty minutes, you know."

Lebutkin just kept turning pages.

"Madame Galois said today is the absolute last day."

Lebutkin leafed away like I was elevator music. I quick got out my French book. I'd actually forgotten all about the stupid presentation. How was I going to speak French for five minutes? All I knew by heart was *My name is* and *I'm so glad to meet you.* Maybe I could do a dialogue between twenty people introducing themselves to each other. I tried taking a deep breath, tore a page out of my notebook, checked my watch. I stood up when the bell rang ending first period.

"No standing," Lebutkin said, not moving his eyes from the magazine.

"I have to make a presentation."

"Sit down."

"She said today—"

"Sit down."

I stood there. "My father's a lawyer, you know."

"Then he can afford to pay all your parking tickets."

My mouth fell open, ready to say something, but I just sat back down. Shit. I crossed my arms, felt like I was overheating. How many tickets were there? What was I going to tell Dad? Or Mom, if I wasn't allowed to

graduate because of the stupid French presentation? Or physics. I still might fail physics.
Or math, if I really screwed up the exam.

Pong. Pong. Pong.

Second period. French. How many times
had I daydreamed about my last French
class? About walking out and never having to
speak French ever again in my entire life? I
checked my watch, looked up at Lebutkin's
rules, at the lowercase *i*. He was taking my
life away here. My last day of school, and
Lebutkin was taking it away.

I was sweating now. Wiped my forehead.
I felt like I could hear a clock ticking, but
there wasn't one in the room. I looked back
at the rules and read them again without
thinking. I knew them by heart. I could get
amnesia, and Lebutkin's rules would be what
I'd remember.

He left in the middle of fourth period. "If
you try opening the door, it'll set off my
beeper." He sounded proud, like he'd in-
vented beeper systems, and before he left he
even showed off how it worked, just in case
I didn't believe him. As soon as he touched
the doorknob, the beeper went off.

"What. No electrified fence?"

He left without saying good-bye. I got out
of my chair and went over and studied the

door like I was some sort of electronics genius who was going to figure out how to escape undetected. I had no idea how it worked, how you could get a door to set off a beeper. I looked at Lebutkin's chair. He'd locked his magazines in a filing cabinet. I would've bet he had all sorts of crap in there. Handcuffs, handguns. Hand grenades, maybe. Lebutkin was definitely the type who'd become a postal worker and end up bombing his co-workers.

Pong. Pong. Pong.

Lunch. My stomach growled. I paced the two steps between Lebutkin's chair and the front wall and heard people outside shouting and laughing. They sounded drunk out there. Lebutkin's room was at one end of the senior locker bay, and I would've sworn people were out there ripping their clothes off and covering themselves in mud. Every few seconds I stopped pacing and stared at the door because I couldn't believe it had gotten even louder. It sounded like people were tackling lockers. Flinging them to the ground like rag dolls. Where was Mr. Urthwon? The assistant principals? Lebutkin? What the hell was Lebutkin doing while all this was going on?

I shook my head and sat down in the back row. I grabbed my forehead and remembered this movie where a guy gets through prison by closing his eyes and fantasizing running through fields of flowers with his naked girl-friend. I closed my eyes and gave it a try, but all I could picture was Zoe last night in the gray T-shirt. I pushed my fingers hard against my forehead and tried imagining famous actresses or the models in Matilda's Victoria's Secret catalogs, but I couldn't really see them without having their pictures right there in front of me. Zoe was no problem, Zoe was easy to picture. Standing at the doorway to my room, rubbing her hair with the white towel. Sitting on the side of my bed. Lying down and resting her head on her two little hands.

"Shit."

I jumped up, went back to pacing. It didn't matter. None of this mattered. I knew none of this was any big deal, knew Sonny was down in the real jail, getting really arrested. This was nothing. This was Lebutkin being jerk-for-a-day. I wasn't going to be finger-printed. I wasn't going to get locked up behind bars. I wasn't going to have a *record*. Getting stuck here with Lebutkin was just a pain in the ass. It was just adolescent. Sonny was right. Our lives were *just* adolescent.

Up until he got dragged away by the police.

Lunch ended and Lebutkin came back. I was sitting up in the first row again, reading a novel I was supposed to have returned to Mrs. Blaffer back in April. It was pretty good. Better than going to English. Plus now I didn't have to cut physics to avoid Zoe. This was the perfect hiding place.

"How long do I get to stay in here after school?" I asked, turning sideways in my seat to look back at Lebutkin. He had another magazine. "Is it OK if I just hang out for a while, close the door behind me?"

Lebutkin stopped turning pages and pretended to read. I think he was trying to figure out if this was a trick.

"There's nothing to steal."

"No talking," Lebutkin finally decided.

"If I break something, you'll know who did it, right?"

"Quiet."

I sat there, watching Lebutkin. "I don't suppose I could drive down to Burger King."

"Shut up."

I turned back around in my seat and grabbed my book. The bell rang to end sixth period, start seventh. I checked my watch and told Lebutkin I had to go to the bathroom. He ignored me.

"Hello?"

"Two minutes."

I walked fast to the bathroom, then made a run for it to the vending machines in the cafeteria and bought a Milky Way bar. God, it was delicious. I could have done a commercial for them, had the whole thing chewed and swallowed by the time I got back to Lebutkin's room.

"You have a visitor," he said, but I was already staring at her sitting there in the seat next to mine.

"What—" I looked at Lebutkin. "I can have *visitors?*"

Without looking up, he held a note out to me. It was from Mr. Lindsey, claiming this was an emergency, that I had to be tutored for the final exam in physics.

I looked over at Zoe. She was sitting straight ahead, staring at the wall. Her arms were resting on a cardboard box the size of a small suitcase sitting on her desk.

"Get to work," Lebutkin said.

I walked over. Sat down. Crossed my arms. Stared straight ahead. We probably looked like we were watching a movie together.

"Sonny says thanks."

My head turned.

"Mrs. Castle refused to press charges. One of the cops mentioned to her what you said about Carey knowing Derrick all the way back in January, and she asked Carey about it."

"In front of everybody?"

"When Carey admitted it, her mom was so mad, she walked out and left Carey there, crying."

"Sonny saw all this?" I was almost salivating, wanted to make sure I had the right picture in my mind.

Zoe nodded. "They drove them both back here in the same squad car."

"Are you serious?"

"Sonny sat in the front seat, and Carey sat in the back."

"Did they talk?"

"Sonny didn't mention it."

"Did the cops tell Mr. Urthwon?"

"I imagine they had to tell him something about why they were bringing Sonny back to school."

"So Urthwon knows about Carey?"

Zoe gave me a look. "Are you worried about her getting the citizenship award?"

"They should at least know what she's really like."

"Your best friend was just released from jail, and you're worried about a meaningless citizenship award?"

"She doesn't deserve it."

"Is it going to change your life?"

"What. It's a matter of being fair."

"What about *your* life?"

"What about it?"

Zoe shook her head and pushed the cardboard box over to my desk. "This was going to be for you."

I held my hands away from the box like it was contaminated. "What is it?"

"It's due back Monday by eleven."

"What is it?"

"A tuxedo," Zoe said, looking down at her desk. "And a prom ticket. I thought it'd be fun if Sonny and you and I all went."

"To the *prom*? You thought the *three* of us could go to the prom?"

"I thought it'd be fun."

"How could it be fun?"

"Never mind."

"You thought the three of us were going to slow-dance together? Sonny and I could be your *entourage*?"

"Drop it, will you?"

"And afterward all *three* of us could sleep together."

Zoe looked wide-eyed, like I was some car about to run her down.

"You don't get it, do you," I said.

Zoe turned. "You're telling me *I* don't get it?"

"Stop playing with me."

"You think I'm playing?"

"Don't. Just don't, OK?"

"You think I'm *playing?*"

"Look. Zoe. I like you. All right?"

"Look. Hale. I'm pregnant. All right?"

chapter

19

～ My arm was in the refrigerator when the phone rang. It couldn't be her. She wasn't about to call. She'd been so mad she'd started to cry. No way would she call. I grabbed another beer and stood up, not looking at the phone, sure it couldn't be her.

Riiiing.

One more and the machine would pick up. Shit. I hated split-second decisions. My hand went for the phone but then stopped. Hell with it. If it was someone else, I didn't want to talk. Chat. Babble. And if it was her, what was I going to say?

Riiiing.

The machine picked up. I strolled into the dark of the family room and looked over at the sliding glass doors, waiting for Dad's voice to stop.

"...sorry we missed your call. Please leave a message."

Beeeep.

I held my breath.

Dial tone.

Shit. I drank some beer, walking back into the kitchen. It never occurred to me that whoever it was wouldn't leave a message, that I wouldn't have any idea who called. What if it *was* her? I drank more beer, mad at myself for not picking up the stupid phone. So I didn't know what to say. So what? So I didn't have to talk. I could've just held the phone to my ear and listened to what *she* had to say.

"Idiot."

I sat down at the kitchen table, looked at the box on the table with the tuxedo inside. Lebutkin wouldn't let me go give it back to her. She'd run out of his room, tears flying, and when I went chasing after her, Lebutkin'd stopped me at the door, smiling like he hoped I'd try to shove him out of the way.

My eyes lost focus as I tapped the top of the box with my fingers. I hadn't opened it, almost like I was afraid there were plastic explosives inside. I looked down at my wrist, but I'd taken off my watch and had stuck it in my pocket, tired of checking. I looked over my shoulder at the clock on the wall. They were dancing by now, probably. Or sitting at their table, trying to talk over the music and staring at the candle in one of those glass bulbs with the fishnetting around it.

They weren't a thing, Zoe and Sonny. They'd never been a thing—not even close. I'd found Sonny in the parking lot after school; he was surprised I even asked about it, kept shaking his head and blinking and staring off into space.

"Not Zoe," he said.

I just stared, my mouth open. He was still stupid about Carey. After she called the police, even after finding out about cheating on him, he still liked her. I wanted to shake him. Idiot. He was an idiot.

"I think Zoe likes *you*."

My head moved forward. "What?"

He shrugged. "That's what it seems like."

"Sonny." I didn't believe it. But even if I *did* believe it, I couldn't understand why he was bringing it up now. "Didn't she tell you—?" I pointed at my stomach. "Do you know she's—?"

"Pregnant. I know."

"Then why are you telling me this? Why even say it?" I could have hit him. Getting me to think Zoe and I could've been a thing. Might've been a thing.

I held my breath, could hear the rain outside.

The phone rang. I didn't even think about it, tripped over my chair.

"Hello?"

"Hi, Haley." It was Matilda, talking loud, music in the background. She had to be calling from Tracy's concert. "Can you hear me?"

I thought of hanging up, but she would've called back.

"Hello? Haley? Are you there?"

"Zoe told me," I said. Matilda was quiet. I sipped some beer, listening to the music playing up there in New York. It wasn't Memento Mori; had to be the warm-up band. I couldn't believe my little sister had a warm-up band.

"I'm glad you know," Matilda said, finally.

"You couldn't have warned me?"

"Hale. It was confidential. You know that."

"You couldn't *hint*? You couldn't even give me a *hint*? A *clue*?"

"I told her I thought she should let you and Sonny know."

I drank some beer.

"It's good she told you. It shows real courage."

"Yeah."

"It also shows she trusts you."

"Right." Matilda didn't say anything, like she was listening, waiting for me to open up. I sipped some more beer.

"It's fortunate she has money," Matilda said eventually. "She can still go to college. Her parents can pay for day care. A nice place to live, with a yard, maybe."

I rolled my eyes. No wonder Sonny was driving her down to Anderson to look at off-campus housing. It wasn't exactly going to be easy, finding a place for a college kid with a baby. I doubted many people would want to share a house with her.

"How's she doing?" Matilda asked.

"How should I know?"

"Did you have a fight?"

I looked at the clock on the wall. "She's at the prom."

Another silence. I could hear applause in the background, could picture Matilda's eyes blinking as she tried to think. "With whom?"

"That's not the point," I said, impatient, not wanting to get into it.

"Is it someone you know?"

"It doesn't matter, OK? I don't care who she went to the prom with. She's pregnant!" I turned away, couldn't believe I'd said it, I'd actually used the word. Just saying it, just hearing it, made it worse.

"I know she's pregnant," Matilda said. "Being pregnant doesn't mean she ceases to exist."

"OK, OK."

"She still matters, Hale."

"O-*K*."

More silence. What was Matilda doing up there? Praying? "I think she cares about you."

"Oh, give me a—" I tried chugging my beer. Sonny was bad enough. Now *Matilda*.

"She didn't say anything explicitly, so I'm not even sure I'm right, but I really think you're very important to her."

Beer spilled out of the side of my mouth. I wiped my chin.

"She seems like a very nice girl, Haley."

I pulled the phone away from my head and looked at it. Was Matilda trying to set me up with a pregnant girl? What were these people thinking?

"I'm sure it felt strange when she told you."

Strange? What was she talking about,

strange? "Matilda— Don't you— You— It makes her this completely different person."

"It doesn't have to."

"Yeah. Right."

"She's still Zoe."

"With this—*baby* growing inside her."

"You make it sound like a disease."

"Don't you—?" I shook my head. "It's great for you. And Dad. But I'm eighteen years old."

"So is she."

"Not anymore."

"She needs her friends right now."

"Yeah. Well . . ."

"Hale?"

"What."

Matilda didn't say anything.

"I should go to the bathroom," I told her. " 'Bye."

I quick hung up the phone like someone was about to jump out of the broom closet and stop me. I looked around, feeling like I'd forgotten something. A thesis paper. An exam. Something important, something ominous, something I'd pay for if I couldn't remember what it was. This was always happening to me. Even after Dad got me the little notebook so I could write things down, I'd still lose track.

The windows were all closed because of the rain, and the kitchen felt hot, clammy. I gulped some beer and tried taking a deep breath, but it felt like all the air had been used up. I wiped sweat off my forehead and walked out to the front hall closet and grabbed Dad's big golf umbrella with the cracked wooden handle. Back in the family room I pushed open the sliding glass door. The rain was louder than I expected, especially when I popped the umbrella open and stepped outside underneath it. The deck shone with rain and felt cold on my bare feet. The backyard was dark, but there was light coming out through the kitchen window and from other houses over fences and through trees. Enough light to see a psychopathic killer before he actually stuck the knife through my heart. I shivered. You see that kind of thing all the time in movies, but it's different imagining it happening to your own body.

The rain fell harder and started to sound like applause. I stared out into the darkness and felt goose bumps, picturing Tracy up in New York walking out onstage in front of thousands of people. They'd have her in some tight, slutty outfit, but then she'd gently walk up to the microphone and start singing and thousands of guys would stop ogling and just sit there and listen.

I couldn't believe I wasn't up there. What was I thinking? What was wrong with me? I could be backstage, looking out at Tracy under all those lights, listening to her voice amplified, echoing out into an enormous, crowded cave of space. Why didn't I go? What was I doing? A psychopathic killer could be lurking out here, about to sneak up and tear my guts out with his bare hands. A meteor could fall out of the sky and land on top of me. The house could explode because I'd accidentally left the oven on. I could be dead, gone, like that. And I was standing here doing nothing. I was spending the weekend worrying about physics. Watching television. God, what was I thinking, watching *television?* While people were out there pinning on corsages. Becoming rock stars. Dancing. Laughing. Holding each other. Eating doughnuts.

I felt a rush of shivers, like I'd seen something out there in the shadows. There *was* something. Standing there, listening to the rain, I suddenly got a feeling there was something. It wasn't anything I could point to and say *There,* but there was *something.* Something I hadn't noticed, hadn't paid any attention to. Something about life, something going on that people would talk about all the time, if they ever found the right words.

I took a deep breath. Exhaled.

Sonny was right. That whole thing about dying—I didn't even know what he was right about, besides the fact that we were all going to die, and I wasn't sure I could even talk to him about it, but there was something he knew, something he was right about. What'd he say, anyway? I hadn't been paying attention, couldn't remember a thing.

I tilted the umbrella and checked the sky for meteors. It would've been great if a flaming meteor came shooting down, crushing the end of the deck, missing me by inches. I could stand here, watching the thing sizzle in the rain, stunned by my luck. What would I do? If a meteor really did come crashing down and missed me by inches, what would I do? I stared at the deck, imagining a smoking meteor sitting there. I'd want to go up to New York. Call an airline and make a reservation for tomorrow. Matilda had written down the name of the hotel and had stuck it under the banana magnet on the refrigerator. I could take a cab from the airport and surprise everybody.

I looked around the backyard, thinking,

wondering. What would I do tonight? If a meteor slammed into the deck at my feet, what would I do tonight?

I took another deep breath and felt my shoulders slide back to normal like I was some kind of cured hunchback. I knew what I'd do. Knew instantaneously, before I even asked myself.

I'd go to the prom.

Talk to Sonny. Ask him about his bullet. Talk to him about death and dying.

Talk to Zoe. Ask her how she felt. Talk to her some more. Dance with her. Tell her I love her.

I got wet trying to shake out the umbrella before I went back inside. I pushed open the sliding glass door, turned on some lights, ran my fingers through my hair. It felt strange, taking my clothes off in the kitchen and trying on the tuxedo. I panicked when the shirt had no buttons, but then I found the little metal things you're supposed to use instead. The whole thing fit great, actually. Mr. Ahm knew what he was doing.

I walked into the bathroom and watched myself sip some beer. I needed to call a taxi. I didn't feel drunk, but I didn't want to drive and find out I was wrong.

I walked back into the family room and grabbed the Yellow Pages off the cookbook shelf and started leafing through, looking for taxis.

Bing-bong.

My eyes shot up, like a thief, caught. Zoe? No, it couldn't be Zoe. I looked at my wrist, but my watch was in my pocket on the floor in the kitchen. Psychopathic killer? Why would he ring the doorbell? Pizza? Maybe Matilda felt sorry for me and ordered one from New York.

Bing-bong. Bing-bong.

Maybe it *was* Zoe. No, it wasn't Zoe. Zoe wouldn't drive all the way over here halfway through the prom. I stood up quietly and walked softly down the hallway.

Bing-bong.

I jumped.

Bing-bong. Bing-bong. Bing-bong.

I quick pulled the door open all at once to get it over with.

A woman stood there. Soaking wet hair. Mrs. Mudd. Zoe's mom.

I looked at her with my mouth open.

"Are you the father?" Her eyes were on fire. If she'd had a gun, she would've shot me.

I started shaking my head. "No."

She watched me a few seconds. Then her shoulders collapsed, the fire went out.

"What's wrong?"

Mrs. Mudd stared past me at nothing. "She's losing the baby."

chapter

20

～ I forgot the umbrella but didn't feel like I could go back for it with Mrs. Mudd walking ahead of me across the front yard like she didn't realize it was raining. She'd left the car running, the headlights on. I climbed in on my side and closed the door and watched the windshield wipers, hoping Mrs. Mudd wouldn't start talking.

"She's bleeding," she'd said, back at the house, while I was sitting on the stairs, tying my shoes. She hadn't been looking at me and might've even forgotten I was there, but I nodded my head anyway, remembering Matilda. When Dad came up to my room last year and told me Matilda was bleeding and they were going to the hospital, I thought she'd cut herself. I jumped off my bed, didn't understand why Dad wasn't running, why he wasn't out of breath, why his voice was sad and solemn instead of panicky.

"It's the baby," he had to tell me.

This time I understood. This time I knew how it worked, and when we got into the car I crossed my arms and didn't want to talk about it.

"Zoe asked me to call you before I drove over," Mrs. Mudd said, taking a left on Pleasant, "but there was no answer."

"I thought it might be her," I said, watching the wipers.

Dad and Matilda had decided it'd be better for me and Tracy to stay home, but Tracy insisted on going to the hospital, so I felt like I should go, too. The waiting room chairs were orange plastic and all faced in one direction, toward a television that was too loud. I tried to ignore it but kept hearing the laugh track. Tracy slouched down in her chair and went into that trance she can do. A black guy tried to turn the TV down, but the volume knob was gone. Dad came out a couple of times to tell us they were waiting to use a machine that would show them what was happening. He looked hopeless. The second time he came out he knelt down on one knee in front of us to talk. Tracy grabbed his hand in both of hers, and he nodded his head, not looking at either one of us. The third time he came out, Letterman was on. Dad was moving slowly, and when he got near us, he opened his mouth to talk, but then shut it. Tracy stood up and put her arms around him, and Dad's eyes closed. The studio audience burst out laughing. Dad whispered.

"They say it happens all the time but . . . We never . . . We just assumed . . ."

The rain fell harder, and Mrs. Mudd turned the wipers on high so they slapped back and forth like they were angry. In the headlights the rain looked like snow.

"I wanted her to get an abortion," Mrs. Mudd said. I stared straight ahead, not trying to think of anything to say, not listening for more.

I only saw Matilda cry once afterward. It was about a month later and she was curled up on the couch, reading a book. Dad tried putting his arms around her as she kept gasping sobs.

"I know," he said. "I know, I know, I know."

I went up to my room. They both knew I

didn't want them having this baby . . . Since the miscarriage I hadn't been able to really look at either one of them.

Mrs. Mudd pulled into the emergency room parking lot and swung into a space. She shut off the ignition and the wipers stopped diagonally across the windshield. I reached for my door but realized Mrs. Mudd hadn't moved. I waited. The rain pounded on the roof, insistent, and reminded me of a fairy tale I thought I remembered where someone couldn't stop knocking on a door.

A lamppost on her side dropped a pale light on her hands, resting on the steering wheel. I cleared my throat. "Mrs. Mudd?"

"I had no idea," she said, quietly.

My eyes ran along the dashboard.

"I had absolutely no idea."

I chewed on my lip. We were facing the emergency room entrance, and I stared across at it and noticed the white limousine parked along the curb. God. I turned away. The limousine made it all seem a lot more real than it had been. I could picture them leaving the prom, Sonny running ahead and scaring the chauffeur and grabbing the umbrella and holding it for Zoe, who must have been—I didn't know. I didn't know what Zoe would do, how she'd respond to this.

"Zoe's dad said he'd be on the next flight." Mrs. Mudd sounded like she was remembering a dream from childhood. "His job requires . . . a lot of travel."

"Should we . . . ?"

Mrs. Mudd nodded slowly. The rain was full of thick, meaty drops, but we walked slowly, Mrs. Mudd still looking like she was trying to remember something. The entrance was brighter than I remembered, but over to the left, in the waiting room, were the orange chairs, still facing the same direction. Mrs. Mudd walked up to the counter, and I stood there by myself. A Hispanic family—mom, dad, three kids—were sitting in the first row of chairs; only the littlest kid was watching the television, which didn't sound quite as loud as the last time. The middle kid, a girl, stared at me like I was famous. What. I checked my fly, saw the tuxedo. I was wearing a tuxedo.

"He's the father," Mrs. Mudd said, her voice out of patience. The little fat nurse sitting behind the counter looked up from her computer, over at me, and then to Mrs. Mudd.

"But when she came in—"

"That was her date to the prom. Look, it's a long story. Can we talk about it later?"

Why was Mrs. Mudd—? I froze, my heart thumping. She wanted me to go back with her, wanted me to see Zoe. Maybe she thought I *wanted* to see Zoe. "Mrs. Mudd?" I walked toward her, pointing toward the waiting room. "I really— I don't think— I'm not—"

Her head snapped toward me. I looked away, guilty.

"Through the doors," the nurse said. "Straight back. Room Three."

"Thank you." Mrs. Mudd turned and walked without looking back for me. I followed her through the electric double doors, my heart going like mad. The emergency room looked just like on television, only no one was there. The curtained cubicles were empty except for an old man sitting on a tall bed with his shirt off. His face was long and gummy and flesh sagged off his chest, but his eyes were preoccupied, like he had more important things to worry about than sitting on a bed in an emergency room. He looked up and stared at me, studied me, like he was considering me for some high-level position. I actually slowed down, thinking he was going to say something. A woman in hospital green was pushing a cart with a machine that looked like it had a pair of lungs. I swallowed, everything seeming to slow down and speed up at the same time. I wasn't ready. I thought I was going to be in the waiting room. I thought I'd hear later, secondhand. I wasn't ready to be here, wearing this stupid tuxedo. The lady in green smiled at me as she went by. The smile was so friendly I thought maybe she recognized me from when I was a little boy, back in New York. It all seemed quieter than it should have, like we were in the middle of a snowstorm. I remembered Sonny telling me how things are bigger than we realize and felt OK about it, but then looked up. Mrs. Mudd was standing in front of Room 3, and I held my breath as she opened the door. The room was dark and closet-sized and crowded with people and a machine with a green radar scope. Sonny looked over as we stepped in, his eyes shining in the light falling in from behind us. Sheets billowed up like a tent at the foot of the bed, and I saw a bare foot up in the air and quickly looked away, at Zoe's face, her eyes wide on the machine as she lifted herself up on her elbows.

"Is that it? Is that it?"

"That's it," a woman standing at the machine said, her face green from the screen.

"Please," said another woman from behind

the door, pushing me into Mrs. Mudd as she slowly closed the door.

"That's my baby?"

"That's your baby."

Zoe looked like she was choking. "Mom."

"Right here."

"That's the heartbeat. That right there. That's it."

"I see it."

"That's my baby."

"I know."

Zoe's eyes were wide and full and stared without blinking at the screen.

"Everything seems fine," the woman standing there said.

"My baby."

"We'll want to monitor you for the next couple of days, and you shouldn't be dancing at any proms for a while, but I think things look good."

Zoe lay back, her head falling against the pillow, her eyes dreamy, still watching the screen.

"I'm sorry, Mom."

"It's going to be OK, Zo."

Zoe's eyes went up to Sonny, then over to me. She looked at the tuxedo for a long time, her eyes filling up again and glancing at my face.

I stood there, didn't look away.